Specky Becky Bucks

JOHN QUINN

POOLBEG

Published 2009
by Poolbeg Press Ltd.
123 Grange Hill, Baldoyle,
Dublin 13, Ireland
Email: poolbeg@poolbeg.com

13 5 7 9 10 8 6 4 2

A catalogue record for this book is available from the British Library.

ISBN 978-1-84223-406-8

Typeset by Patrica Hope in Times New Roman 12.5/17
Cover design and illustrations by Derry Dillon
Printed and bound in Great Britain by
CPI Cox & Wyman, Reading, RG1 8EX

www.poolbeg.com

Praise for Book of the Year Award winning
The Summer of Lily & Esme

"The tone is lyrical and reflective, the narrative compelling and the setting evoked with an excellent sense of contemporary and period detail."

The Irish Times

"This . . . has a touch of magic about it. It is haunting and funny – and you certainly don't have to be a child to enjoy it."

Sunday Press

"An absorbing read . . ."

Evening Press

"It is a rare achievement to portray so convincingly a child's reaching out beyond his own loneliness to share in the fading and disconnected memories of those of a much older generation."

The Irish Times

Specky Becky Bucks

Also by John Quinn

The Summer of Lily & Esme
The Gold Cross of Killadoo
Duck & Swan
One Fine Day

About the author

John Quinn was born in Co Meath and worked as a
teacher before becoming a radio producer for RTÉ. *The
Summer of Lily & Esme* was his first work of fiction.
Other books for children include *The Gold Cross of
Killadoo, Duck & Swan* and *One Fine Day.*

For my beautiful granddaughters
Eva and Georgia
– always follow your dreams.

And with thanks to Lynne,
who gave me the idea.

Specky Becky Bucks

The true story (as told by herself) of
Rebecca Jane Buckley age 9 1/4
known to her friends as Becky Bucks
and to her enemies as Specky Becky Bucks
(guess why!)
whose passion is Gaelic football
and whose dream is to play in Croke Park.

1

All About Me
(well, nearly all . . .)

All right. My name is Rebecca Jane Buckley, aged nine and a quarter. The quarter might not seem important but, when you're not very big, every little bit is important. I am one hundred and four centimetres tall – when my hair is up. Otherwise, when my hair is in a ponytail, I am one hundred and fourteen centimetres. At least it sounds better that way than in feet and inches – which I am not telling anyway. "All About Me" does not have to include feet and inches. All right?

My dad says I am lean and mean. He said that when I kicked him on the shin during a football match in our back garden. He tackled me unfairly from behind. It was during the World Cup and he had been watching too much television. I gave him a yellow card, as I was also the referee. I also gave him a kick on the shin because he hurt me. I know referees can't do that but I was cross with him. So he gave me a red card and walked off. Or rather limped off. I was really cross with him then because I was leading 1–0. He was so badly injured, he said, that he took the next day off work. Of course that had nothing to do with the fact that his team, Argentina, was playing that afternoon, he said.

Most of the time my dad is cool. His name is David but nearly everyone calls him Dave. He works in IT. Computer stuff. My mother is Margaret but no-one ever calls her that. She is Mags. She is Mum to me of course but to the rest of world – most of whom she seems to know – she is Mags. She is quite tall (where they got me I do not know, but Dad says it was the last day of the sale. That's Dad trying to be really cool. Not.) and always keeps her hair cut short. She doesn't need to put it up like me. She goes to the gym to work out once a week, but she doesn't play football. She works three days a week in 'Dazzling Interiors.' They sell sofas.

But this is supposed to be all about me – right? My name is Rebecca Jane Buckley, but of course nobody calls me that. Becky, my friends call me. Becky Bucks. I don't mind really. I mean – is anyone ever called by their real name? Victoria is Vicky. Kelly is Kells. Deirdre is Dee.

The only people that call me Rebecca are:
1. My teacher Miss Lane (also known as Boreen – you know, "little road." Boreen – Boring – get it?) "Rebecca, I don't seem to have your homework here . . ." "And the name of Ireland's longest river? Who can tell me? Rebecca?" ("The Shannon, Miss." I knew that because Mum's name was Shannon before she married Dad. Margaret Shannon – "I was so famous, they named a river after me," she says. That was funny the first time I heard it.)

2. Granny Shannon. She lives in London, so I don't see her too often. And she's not well just now. But on the phone it's always "And how is darling Rebecca? Such a lovely name for a lovely girl. I hope they're not calling you Becky. I don't like that, Rebecca. Of course I wanted to call you Marguerita, but then I suppose they would call you Rita." RITA??? Grandad Shannon calls me Becky. He's cool.

3. Mrs Pratt next door. She must be as old as Granny Shannon – at least. I won't say anything about her name, but when I get in trouble for kicking my ball

3

over the hedge (which is often) the voice rings out, "Rebecca! You've damaged my hydrangeas again!" (Hydrangeas are flowers, Dad says. Mrs Pratt lives for her hydrangeas, he says. I don't understand that.) "Please try to control your football, Rebecca," Mrs Pratt says. Sometimes the ball comes back punctured. "I'm afraid Scotty got to the ball first, Rebecca," Mrs Pratt says. "He's such a playful thing." He is the Pratts' terrier. Imagine being called Scotty Pratt. I hate Scotty Pratt. And he's so OLD he couldn't even burst a bubble. He certainly couldn't bite a hole as big as – as big as one made by a BREAD KNIFE. A lot of the time the ball never comes back. Somewhere in the darkness of the Pratts' coal-cellar I imagine an amazing collection of balls – footballs, beachballs, sponge balls, tennis balls – MY balls! And when Mrs Pratt dies . . . but Dad says I should NOT TALK LIKE THAT and anyway Mrs Pratt is right, he says. You need to improve your ball control. He says this as he trips himself up trying to do fancy stuff. I say nothing.

The only time the ball really comes back – undamaged – is when Mr Pratt finds it. He likes to head the ball over the hedge. He giggles but doesn't say anything, putting his finger to his lips.

I can't wait for that hedge to grow, to keep my balls on the right side.

4. Sometimes Mum calls me Rebecca – like in the supermarket – "Rebecca, where are you?" or when she collects me from school – "Rebecca, over here!" That's okay, but I *hate* when she calls me "Becksy-Wecksy." She usually does this to tease me and she tickles me at the same time. "How's my little Becksy-Wecksy?" She makes me feel about *one* and a quarter.

What I really absolutely and totally DETEST is being called "Specky Becky." You know why, of course. Spectacles, glasses. For as far back as I can remember I have had to wear them. They are "corrective," Mum says. Eventually I won't need them, she says. But how long is eventually? Forever, it seems to me. They are funny glasses. All bendy and plastic. You can turn them and twist them this way and that. Which is just as well when there are people like Simon about. (I'll tell you about Simon later). I have to wear the glasses all the time. I suppose I am used to them now. "All the time" includes playing football. Some people think that is strange – or even funny.

"Go Specky!" they shout. "Go Specky Becky!"

I suppose I am used to that too. I suppose. It's not a problem for me, playing football with glasses. It's a problem for some others. The only time it bothers me is when it rains. I wish I had little windscreen wipers then. Swish! Swish! they would go. And I could see the ball – and the goals. Which reminds me – but I'll tell you about that later too. For now, that's enough about me. I must go outside and improve my ball control (Mr Pratt is working in his garden).

My name is Rebecca Jane Buckley. My friends call me Becky Bucks. Some people call me . . . never mind! And I love football.

2

More About Me, Actually

To be exact, I love Gaelic football. I'm the only one in our house who does. Dad says it is a mystery. He says there was nothing on the label about Gaelic football when they bought me at the end of sale bargains. Ha! Ha! He says he first noticed my interest in football when I kicked the rattle out of my pram. Mum says I was probably telling him to change my nappy. Mum knows why I'm a Gaelic footballer. It's in the blood, she says.

All the Shannons were great footballers, Mum says. "Except me, of course. Girls didn't play football then. My dad Jimmy was the best of all. He played for Meath. In Croke Park."

Croke Park! Grandad Shannon played in Croke Park! My dream is to play in Croke Park.

"Did they win, Mum?"

"I wouldn't know," Mum laughs. "It happened before I was born!"

"That long ago?" Dad is trying to be funny again.

Mum steps on his toe. "Yes, David. THAT ('OUCH!') long ago. Next time we see him you can ask him."

Next time . . . We don't see Grandad much now that Granny Shannon is not well.

"Wait a minute!" Mum exclaims. "The photograph!" She goes rooting in the sideboard.

"What photograph, Mum?"

"Shush! Patience!"

At last she pulls an album from the third drawer. She flicks through the pages. "There! I knew I had it!"

It's a newspaper cutting. A photograph of a small (very small) baby, sitting in a huge silver cup. The paper is dated 30th September 1999.

"Read what it says underneath," Mum says. She stands on Dad's toe again. "OUCH!"

I read it very slowly.

"One-year-old Rebecca Buckley looks none too happy as her grandfather, former Meath footballer Jimmy Shannon, raises her aloft in the Sam Maguire Cup during the homecoming celebrations following Meath's All-Ireland victory."

ME! That bawling baby with the scrunched up face is ME! I am so embarrassed.

"Yes," Mum purrs. "That's my little Becksy-Wecksy!"

"Mum!" I am even more embarrassed.

"And mine!" adds Dad, stepping well away from Mum.

But how? Why? Why ME?

"Grandad came home for the All-Ireland Final. He was so excited when Meath won. I had to drive him down to Navan for the celebrations. The first chance he got to hold the cup, he whipped you out of my arms and popped you into the cup. Just in time for the photograph. Poor little Becksy-Wecksy –" *("MUM!")* – "you were so terrified!"

"Probably needed your nappy changed," Dad calls from the safety of the kitchen.

I don't want to think about that. I am so embarrassed about that photograph. But that IS me. In the Sam Maguire Cup.

"You see," says Mum. "You were destined to be a football star."

"Anyone for a cup of wee – sorry – tea?" Dad calls.

"Just jealous," Mum whispers as she replaces the album in the drawer.

So that's what Mum means when she says Gaelic football is in my blood. I sat in the Sam Maguire Cup when I was a baby – a very small baby. And I bawled. In case you don't know, the Sam Maguire Cup is the biggest cup you can win in Gaelic football. (And it IS big – big enough to put a very small bawling baby into it). It's presented every September to the county that wins the All-Ireland Final in Croke Park in Dublin. Croke Park is a huge stadium. My dream is to play there. And just think – my grandad played there! It's in the blood, Mum says.

She has just reminded me that she has been in Croke Park too. She went with nine of her pals to see a Robbie Williams concert. Each of them wore a white tee shirt with the words

ROBBIE'S GIRLS ON TOUR SUMMER 2006

printed on it. I was so embarrassed when they went off in three taxis.

"It was fab," Mum says. "The sound was awful. Could hardly see Robbie. But you just had to be there!"

Sorry, Mum. That just doesn't count. You have to be in Croke Park to PLAY FOOTBALL for it to count.

"Fat chance of that ever happening to me," she laughs as she waltzes out to the kitchen singing 'Let

Me Entertain You.' "Too awkward! See! I've just stood on Dad's toe again!"

"OUCH!"

It's time for me to practise my ball control again.

You may be thinking by now that I am a spoiled little only child. You could not be more wrong. I am the (very small) baby of a family of three. Next up – about twenty centimetres up – is my brother, Evan Thomas Buckley. I know what you're thinking. ET Buckley. Please phone home. Lots of times I wish he would – and that the spaceship would come and take him back to the alien planet from which he came. No, really – he's not too bad for a big brother. He did give me football gloves last Christmas after all – but he has absolutely no interest in football, Gaelic or otherwise. Computers, PlayStations – that's ET's world. While I dream of playing in Croke Park he dreams of spending a day in Dad's office. When Dad tried to get him interested in the World Cup, ET agreed to wear a Brazilian shirt with the name *FRED* on it – because he thought the name was cute, not because he knew or cared that "Fred" was a Brazilian striker – and then spent the whole World Cup at his computer. And he doesn't have to wear glasses. Go on, ET – make that call.

And then there is Shona. The BIG SISTER. Shona

lives on another planet – a different one from ET. The MTV planet. Shona is fourteen. She is supposed to be studying for her Junior Cert and she is in love. With Mogsy. She says. Mogsy is seventeen and plays in a garage band called The Forever Undead. Shona believes they will be the next U2. They made a demo tape once which Shona listens to – endlessly. Shona dreams of being The Forever Undead's manager when they are famous. "Fine," Dad says, "but just in case they never make it out of the garage, would you please study so you will have your Junior Cert to fall back on?"

"You just don't understand," Shona wails. "Just you wait. You'll see." And she plays the tape again.

Dad throws his hands in the air. "If you don't do your study, Shona, so help me, I'll make sure that lot will become the Forever Dead!"

Shona likes to wear an Ireland soccer shirt. It has

MOGSY

1

printed on the back. That's the nearest she will ever be to being a football fan.

So what chance have I of ever becoming a football star with

– a Mum who is "too awkward" and prefers to listen to Robbie Williams

– a brother who is from another planet where football has not been discovered yet

– a sister who dreams of touring the world with Mogsy who has spots and lives in a garage

– and a Dad who thinks he can play football but only trips himself up, tackles from behind and anyway hasn't really got the time.

I forgot. There is also Puddles our dog. His name was Patch but when he was a pup I seemed to be always running to tell Mum, "He's doing puddles again!" And Mum would scream, "Oh no – my beautiful rug!" as she grabbed him by the neck, locked him in the garage and gave him a five-minute lecture before sponging her beautiful rug with washing-up liquid. He doesn't do puddles any more – at least not on the rug – but the name stuck. Sometimes he will play ball with me but he gets tired of football after about two minutes and decides to bark at Scotty Pratt. This of course annoys Mrs Pratt and she calls out from the middle of her hydrangeas – "Rebecca! Could you please control that dog of yours! He's upsetting Scotty again."

It's just as well there is Josh.

3

Josh

Josh lives across the road and three houses down – at Number 14, also known as CHATTANOOGA. That's where his family came from – Chattanooga in America. They came to Ireland three years ago.

Josh saw me in the football kit Santa gave me.

"Would you like to come to my garden and play soccerball? I've got goals with a net!"

Soccerball! Americans have some strange words – but he also had goals with a net (and a tree house and a climbing frame and a genuine wigwam – that's a tent) in his garden. How could I refuse? Even if it was a "soccerball" goal and not a Gaelic football goal.

"I'll have to ask my Mum," I said.

Mum of course thought it was a wonderful idea and off we went to play soccerball at Chattanooga.

Josh

Josh is actually quite good at soccer. When he was five he had a soccerball coach at his school in America. He's not too keen on Gaelic football but I'm his coach now. We made an agreement. When I play "away" (in his garden) we play soccer and when I play "home" (in my garden) we play Gaelic football. Of course we play mostly in his garden, because he has proper goals – with a net. In our stadium we have to make do with the washing-line pole and the scraggy little apple tree that Dad planted and that never produced an apple. With a hedge for a net. And Mrs Pratt for a referee who won't give back the ball every time Josh gives it one of his wild kicks – which is often.

There are other rules. No home games on Monday. It's washday and Mum got tired of re-washing clothes with football prints on them. No away games on Wednesday. Josh's Mum has her meditation group around on a Wednesday. They do chanting stuff in the garden. Weird.

Josh is ten. I like him a lot. He's good fun, even if he uses strange words like soccerball, sidewalk (footpath) and sneakers (runners). And buddies. "You're my ball-buddy," Josh says. He means football-friend. And he's right of course. Except that Shona wouldn't leave it at that.

"Here come Josh and Becks," she sneers.

Posh and Becks – Josh and Becks – get it? Ha. Ha. Ha. How pathetic is that? Shona can be really annoying at times. I can be really cross at times.

"Here come Shona and Spotsy," I snigger.

Shona complains to Mum like the big baby she is and I go into hiding – in Josh's garden actually – but it works, for a while.

I have the whole football kit, including wristbands and headband. The jersey is special. Dad got it for me in London. He says he used to follow Tottenham Hotspur when he was a boy. He liked the name – thought it was cute, just like ET with Fred. Last year he went on a business trip. He was taken to White Hart Lane to see a Tottenham match and to meet the players. Lucky duck! So quick-thinking Dad runs into the Spurs Shop, buys a Robbie Keane shirt and gets Robbie to sign it for his beloved daughter Becky. At times like this Dad can be really cool. So what if the shirt almost reaches my ankles. So what if Robbie's signature is a blue splotch down near the tail. It's a Tottenham shirt, signed by Robbie and it's mine.

That's football at home. Football at school is something else. Once a week Miss Lane brings us out to the field – or our *quarter* of the field, as there are three other classes out at the same time. She throws a few footballs to us and tells us not to run into one another. Boreen.

At least that's how it was until Mr Long, the principal, made a very important announcement when we came back to school last September after the summer holidays. Every time Mr Long makes an announcement over the school radio system I get worried as it is usually bad news.

"ATTENTION PLEASE! The toilets in Room 5 are blocked – again – and, for the time being, Room 5 will use the toilets in Room 6. Thank you."
or
"ATTENTION PLEASE! Please have all your tickets for the School Fund raffle sold by NEXT MONDAY and bring all the money in on that day. Thank you."

For once, the news was just brilliant.

4

The Coach

"ATTENTION PLEASE! I'd like to welcome a new member to our teaching staff. He is Mr O'Sullivan and he will be taking Fifth Class in Room 10. Apart from being an excellent teacher, Mr O'Sullivan is mad about Gaelic football. He's from Kerry, you see, and they're all mad in Kerry – mad about Gaelic football. That was my little joke, Mr O'Sullivan. He is very anxious to develop our school teams at under-eight, under-ten and under-twelve. We are very lucky to have Mr O'Sullivan as he was very successful with teams in his previous school and let's face it – this school hasn't exactly set the world on fire with any of its teams in recent years."

There was a pause. I didn't even KNOW we had teams

in our school before now. Miss Lane was about to continue the Irish Reading class when Mr Long took off again.

"So this week Mr O'Sullivan is arranging a series of trials for under-eights, under-tens and under-twelves. And he says he wants everybody out. Even if you never kicked a ball before. Mr O'Sullivan believes everyone should have a chance and I agree with him. All it will mean is a short little game – ten minutes with teams of five-a-side. If teachers will kindly submit their class lists to Mr O'Sullivan, he will organise the teams. I hope that's clear to everyone. Five-a-side. Ten minutes. Everyone gets a chance."

Another pause. Miss Lane took a big breath, but Mr Long still wasn't finished.

"So this afternoon, Monday, under-eights out on the field after lunch. Everyone. Wednesday afternoon, under-tens. Everyone. Friday afternoon, under-twelves. Everyone. Be there and be a player! Heh! Heh! Once again thanks to Mr O'Sullivan. I hope everyone will give him full co-operation. Apologies for the length of this bulletin. It will be repeated at twelve thirty. Thank you."

Miss Lane rolled her eyes to heaven and finally got the Irish Reading under way.

"Anois! Tá Pól agus Peigí sa charr."

Trials! A chance for everyone. Brill! Under-tens on Wednesday. I'll show Mr O'Sullivan how brilliant I am. I'll probably score a few goals. Go on a solo run. I'm good at that. Probably save a few certain goals –

"Rebecca? *Lean leat!* Rebecca! Would you please continue?"

Miss Lane's voice startles me. I haven't a clue where we are in the reading but Tracy sneaks her finger across the page to help me out. Thanks, Trace.

"Maith . . . an . . . cailín, Peigí . . ." I stumble along.

"Agus maith an cailín, Tracy," Miss Lane says in her Boreen voice. "This is Irish Reading time, Rebecca. Dreaming is for bedtime."

"Yes, Teacher."

The morning drags on. In the afternoon, I manage to get a peep at the under-eight trials whenever Teacher is writing on the blackboard. Mr O'Sullivan is running around with a whistle in his mouth and a clipboard in his hand. He waves his arms and stops now and then to write on his clipboard. The little ones (most of them are bigger than me, actually) are running around and bumping into one another. It all seems very exciting. I can't wait until –

WHOOSH! The blinds shoot down and give me a fright.

"Dreaming is for bedtime, Rebecca," says a voice from the corner of the room.

I can't wait until Wednesday afternoon.

5

Five-a-Side

Wednesday afternoon did come – after about two years. That's what it seemed like anyway. We all piled out onto the field, chattering and tricking.

"QUIET!" roared Mr O'Sullivan. He has a VERY strong voice. "It's very important that you listen to me when I call out the teams. I'll only do it once. If you don't come, you don't play. It's very important that you listen to me ALL THE TIME. Is that clear?"

We sort of nod, most of us. "IS THAT CLEAR?" he roars.

"YES, MR O'SULLIVAN," we roar back.

He picks the first two teams. My name doesn't come up. The rest of us watch the first game. Mr O'Sullivan moves the goalposts quite near each other. The pitch is quite small, but then there are only five on each team. Mr O'Sullivan roars and waves his arms.

"Kick it, Samantha! With your foot – not your knee!"

"Pick it UP, Darren. It won't bite you!"

"I KNOW the ball is dirty, Tracy!"

This is too easy. Please let me be on the next team so I can show Mr O'Sullivan how brilliant I am . . .

The whistle blows.

"Right. Thank you. Now, next game. Listen for your names. Are you LISTENING?"

"Rebecca Buckley . . ."

I'm on! It's showtime! I skip forward, little knowing the disaster that lies ahead.

"Rebecca! You should have been here on Monday. Under-eights."

"I'm nine and a quarter," I growl.

"Well, that's a bit of bad luck," Mr O'Sullivan sighs. "However, we'll move on."

Not a very good start, but he hasn't seen me play yet. I'm in at Number One. Then the disaster begins.

Number Two is Goodwill. Goodwill came from Nigeria. He is a very friendly boy and he smiles all the time. He is not bad at football but only – as I discover – at soccer. Goodwill does not believe in touching the ball with his hands. No matter how much you tell him, beg him, roar at him – he won't take the ball in his hands. "I can't do that," he says. "It is not right. I can't do that!"

Number Three is Tomasz. Tomasz came from Poland. He is very shy and does not smile at all. To make matters worse, he knows very little English. "Over here, Tomasz!" "Kick it, Tomasz!" "Stand on your head, Tomasz!" "Like an ice-pop, Tomasz?" It's all the same to him. And if someone runs for the ball, Tomasz is too shy to go near him. Great! We now have a player who won't handle the ball and another who is too shy to go near it. And me, of course. Things can only get better. WRONG. Things can only get worse.

Number Four is Saul. What can I say about Saul? What – can – I – say – about – Saul? Saul is a very nice boy. He wears glasses but that's all right. So do I. Except that Saul's glasses are glass glasses not plastic bendy glasses like mine. But the problem with Saul is that he has absolutely NO interest in sport. Not just football. Sport. Absolutely NO interest. Saul's main interest in life is creepy-crawlies. Anything that creeps or crawls. Worms, spiders, beetles, ants. That's our Saul. He got a special prize last year for his project on worms. So why am I surprised that he spends most of the five-a-side match on his hands and knees searching the grass for creepy-crawlies?

"Your ball, Saul!" screams Mr O'Sullivan.

"I'm busy," Saul whispers.

What have I done to deserve a team like this? What have I done – oh, no! Please no. Not her.

Number Five is Storm. I forgot to tell you about Storm. Storm is Josh's sister. That's about the best I can say about Storm. She is the most spoiled child ever. Whatever she wants she gets. Last year she amazed everyone by gliding into school one day. She went on to spend the day gliding – in and out of class, up and down corridors and finally into Mr Long's office. It was our first time to see heelies in action. They were probably the first heelies in Ireland. Mr Long banned heelies from school that day. Storm was not happy. She bawled for a day – until she got some new toy. Storm is very well named.

So why am I surprised that one minute into the game Storm complains to Mr O'Sullivan that no-one will give her the ball? A minute later when the ball sort of fell into her hands, Simon knocked it out again, grabbed it and scored (another) goal against us. Storm went bawling to Mr O'Sullivan. "Did you see that? Did you SEE that? He took the ball from me?"

"It's okay, Storm. He is allowed to do that."

It wasn't okay for Storm.

"He most certainly is not!" she screamed. And with that, after three minutes, Storm walked off the pitch in a huff.

I suppose you could say she stormed off.

6

A Bad Start

We lost. I know that does not surprise you. We lost by fourteen goals and four points to one goal and one point. I will repeat that. We lost by FOURTEEN GOALS AND FOUR POINTS to ONE GOAL AND ONE POINT. By the way, I scored the point. Goodwill scored the goal. At least, when we finally convinced him to use his hands (at the very end of the game) he just THREW the ball into the goals. Mr O'Sullivan said in the circumstances he would allow the goal. The circumstances were that the other team had already scored thirteen goals and four points. And they still had time to score another goal before Mr O'Sullivan blew the final whistle. But I scored the point. It was class. I just did a little solo run and ran around Maria (who was talking to Goodwill at the time) before kicking it over the bar. It was a really cool score. Mr O'Sullivan said so. "Very cool, Rebecca. The comeback starts here."

But it didn't.

When you think about it, it really was something to score eighteen times in ten minutes. Every time we kicked the ball out they came back and scored. They had no wides. Simon scored ten goals and did cartwheels like Robbie Keane each time. Or at least he *tried* to do cartwheels. Usually he fell over in a heap. Mr O'Sullivan was not impressed.

"Arra, get up out of that, Simon, and don't be making a show of yourself!"

It was easy enough for Simon seeing that our goalkeeper, Saul, was on his hands and knees in the goalmouth searching for creepy-crawlies. Saul complained to Mr O'Sullivan that Simon had killed at least one worm and one beetle with his big boots. Mr O'Sullivan made a funny noise and said some strange words.

Saul wasn't the only one to complain. Storm's mother marched into Mr Long's office to complain about the rough games they played in the school.

"My Storm came home with TWO broken nails. Do you know how badly that will damage her modelling career?"

28

A Bad Start

As for Tomasz, at least he knows some English now. "Kick it!" "Run!" "Did you SEE that?" (the last one thanks to Storm). But he's still very shy. Goodwill is getting there. "Are you SURE it's all right to touch the ball?" "Yes, Goodwill, it's all right." He can do a solo run too, thanks to me. Trouble is, he does it all the time, running around in circles, laughing his head off while everyone else is screaming for the ball. Meanwhile Saul is happy just being Saul, exploring the creepy-crawly world. He found a centipede and brought it in to show it to Teacher. She was very nervous about it and when it slid off Saul's hand and into her handbag she was more than nervous. She was HYSTERICAL.

"Get it out! Get it out!" she screamed.

Saul had to empty the handbag very carefully. Tracy nudged me and we giggled as we watched the pile grow on her desk. Tissues, perfume, tablets, mobile, a purse, keys, a hairbrush, sweets (or was it more tablets?) and a photograph in a frame . . .

"Must be Mr Boreen," whispered Tracy. He had a big head of hair and looked very serious.

"Quickly, Saul, quickly," snapped Teacher, looking the other way. Saul took his time.

"I'd say he's a farmer," Tracy giggled.

At last Saul found his beloved centipede.

"Now take it as far away from here as you can," said Teacher, filling up her handbag again. She definitely blushed as she picked up the photograph.

Tracy could not help herself. "Is that –?"

"Maths books, page sixteen, quickly, quickly!" snapped Teacher, dropping the photograph into her bag. She shut her handbag tight and shoved it into the drawer of her desk.

"And what of Becky Bucks?" you may ask.

I decided my football career was over. Never would I be picked for the school team. Never would I win a medal. And certainly never would I run onto Croke Park to the cheering of thousands ("Go, Becky, go!") and dazzle everyone with my amazing speed and skill before being presented with the cup by THE PRESIDENT (photograph in all the newspapers). NEVER. And all because I was unfortunate enough to be picked on a team with Goodwill – and Tomasz – and Saul – and, worst of all, Storm. A team that had FOURTEEN GOALS and FOUR POINTS scored against them in TEN MINUTES. It just wasn't fair. I was so depressed.

A hand touched my shoulder in the playground.

"It's Rebecca, isn't it?"

"Yes, Mr O'Sullivan."

"You were a bit unlucky with your team, weren't you? The international team."

"I suppose so, Mr O'Sullivan."

"But you showed some nice touches. Cheeky solo run. You never stopped trying. And you scored a point!"

He remembered! He remembered all that about me.

"You're in the under-ten squad, Rebecca."

"Sorry?"

"You're in the under-ten squad. Training on Wednesdays. Well done, Rebecca!"

"Thank you, Mr O'Sullivan."

I could not believe it. I was in the squad. I floated through the afternoon in a dream.

"Dreaming is for bedtime, Rebecca!"

Miss Lane must have said that to me five times. I didn't care. I couldn't wait to tell Mum, Dad, Josh – especially Josh.

I was in the squad.

7

The Squad

Mum and Dad were impressed by my news, I suppose. The news that I was in the squad.

"I AM impressed," Mum said, "but I hope my little Becksy-Wecksy won't be hurt?"

NEXT!

"There you go, Becky," Dad said. (Dad says "There you go" a lot). "I knew all those tricks I taught you would work! I have a few more up my sleeve!" (*Thanks, Dad. No, thanks. I don't think I need any new tricks.*)

ET was on a particularly distant planet when I brought home the news. He was not in radio contact with Planet Earth at the time.

And of course I knew what Shona would say.

"And is Josh in the squad too? Josh and Becks. The deadly duo!"

The Squad

She is so pathetic. Of course Josh is not in the squad. He's in the under-twelve squad, silly. He's thrilled about that. His mother isn't. She's still very annoyed about the damage to Storm's modelling career. Storm now wears special gloves to school every day. But at least Josh and I can now do special training at home – because we're in the squads.

I like Mr O'Sullivan. He has a very strong and sometimes a very LOUD voice, but he praises you out loud when you do something well. And when you make a mess of things, he will say, "Come on, Becky. Try again. Next time, Becky. Next time."

When we had our first training session, he asked me to show the others how to do a solo run. So there I was, on my own in front of all the others running up and down – tip the ball with your toe, catch it, tip it, catch it – and keep running all the time.

"Excellent, Becky," Mr O'Sullivan said. "You see, lads –" (we're not all lads – Ciara is in the squad too, but I don't mind) – "that's TALENT! Some have it. Some don't. It's a gift. I don't know where Becky got it, but she has it."

I suppose it's in the blood, like Mum said.

"Anyone could do that!" Simon said.

"Okay, Simon. You do it." Mr O'Sullivan threw the ball to him.

33

Specky Becky Bucks

You remember Simon. Ten-goal Simon. Cartwheel Simon. He started well with the first tip, but as soon as he started running he made a mess of things, kicking the ball over his head, dropping it, kicking it too far ahead – until he tripped himself up and fell in a heap.

"Need to practise, Simon. Need to practise," Mr O'Sullivan said.

I'm nearly sure he winked at me as he said it.

Simon is BIG. He is HUGE. Although he is only nine – well, nearly ten – he is twice the size of me and about ten times heavier. I know that because he fell in a heap (Simon *always* falls in a heap) ON TOP OF ME during one training session. SQUASH! I thought it was the end of the world, or at least the end of me. When Mr O'Sullivan rescued me from under the heap I was so dizzy. Everyone else laughed – especially Simon – but I didn't find it funny. Nor did Mr O'Sullivan. He made me sit in his car, wrapped in his tracksuit top, for the rest of the session. I was all right but I was sore all over for the next two days.

Simon is a bully, on and off the field. Once he tied the laces of Tracy's runners in a big black knot. She had to hop around like a kangaroo until Miss Lane cut the laces with a scissors. Worse than that, he also tied my bendy glasses in a knot. He is that strong. It took Mr Long ages to untie them and straighten them. Mr

The Squad

Long sent for Simon's dad. When I saw him come out of Mr Long's office I knew why Simon is so huge. His dad nearly got stuck in the office door. Simon was quiet for a while but a week later when the plumber discovered that it was Goodwill's woolly hat and scarf that were blocking the toilets of Room 5, everyone KNEW who was to blame, but no-one could prove it. Simon just shrugged his shoulders and smiled his evil smile.

Goodwill continues to smile – all the time. He is slowly getting used to Gaelic football. He has stopped running around in circles and has agreed to share the ball with the rest of us. "I can touch the ball – cool," he keeps saying. Goodwill has a new pair of football gloves. I just hope they don't end up in the toilets of Room 5 . . .

So there we all were, twenty of us, practising our skills in The Paddocks. The farmer kindly moves the cows during training. He's a friend of Mr O'Sullivan's. We practise our kicking skills, our catching skills, our passing skills, our shooting skills. Mr O'Sullivan says we are doing very well. He is trying to arrange a match against another school after the mid-term break – to see how good we are. Actually, I think he said "to see if we are any good" which is not quite the same thing. And Simon still can't do the solo run. Pathetic.

8

A Big Surprise

Just before the mid-term break, Mum made a surprise announcement. Mum likes to tease you before telling you.

"Guess where we're going next week, gang?" No one had a clue but everyone had to guess.

"A Robbie Williams concert?" I suggested, half-joking, half-fearing I might be right.

"Cheeky!" Mum laughed. "I wish . . ."

"On a family hill walk," was ET's guess.

"No, but a good suggestion, ET. I'll keep it in mind."

"Yes," Dad chimed in. "And we can go camping like in my boy scout days. Live in a tent. Lots of family bonding!"

I shivered at the thought, remembering Dad's

pathetic attempt to put up a tent in the garden during the summer. I made a frown at ET. He just shrugged his shoulders and beamed himself off to Planet Zog again. They are welcome to him.

"Not Aunt Rita's, I hope," Shona said with a huge sigh.

For once I agreed with Shona. Aunt Rita lives down the country. She and Uncle Mattie have no children. Aunt Rita runs a Bed and Breakfast business. She has a thing about tidiness. If you bring in a speck of mud on your runners or if you don't screw the cap properly on the toothpaste tube, you are in big trouble. And Uncle Mattie hardly ever talks. The food is nice, though.

"No, not Aunt Rita's – though we are due a visit there."

Two visits in one year? She cannot be serious.

"No. All wrong! We're off to . . ." a long pause ". . . LONDON."

London! This was seriously interesting.

Even ET made a special return from Planet Zog. "Cool!" he whispered. "Yes. Really cool!" I agreed.

For once ET and I were on the same wavelength.

"Well actually – it won't be a very pleasant visit." Mum's voice had changed. "We're going to see Granny Shannon. She's not well."

My heart sank.

Her voice had a tremble now. "She's in hospital and . . ." Dad put his arm around Mum.

"But we can do other things as well," he said. "Go on the London Eye. Help cheer up Grandad."

Of course! Grandad Shannon, who played in Croke Park. My heart lifted again.

Shona was the problem. Not for the first time.

"Well, I'm sorry. I can't go."

"And why would that be?" Dad asked.

"Because – well – I mean – who would look after Puddles?"

"Your interest in Puddles is touching, Shona, but the Brennans have agreed to take him. Now what is the REAL reason?" Dad scratched his chin. Always a bad sign.

"Well – because – if you must know – The Forever Undead are playing their first gig and I promised Mogsy –"

"No way. No-o-o-o way." Dad was scratching his chin furiously now.

"But I'm going to be their MANAGER and I need to be –"

"You need to be packing your bag for London, Shona." Scratch. Scratch.

"You don't understand. You're horrible. I HATE you!"

A Big Surprise

There followed a BIG SCENE. ET and I were sent out of the room but the screams and the sobs told me Shona was putting up quite a fight. And in the end, Shona won, but – as they say on television – terms and conditions apply. Shona would go to the Brennans with Puddles ("no teen parties, Shona") and Mr Brennan would leave her to the gig and collect her ("and it had better be over before midnight, Shona").

As usual, Shona had the last word.

"In five years' time I'll be going to London as manager of The Forever Undead when they will be collecting a major award for their latest album. Just you wait and see!"

More scratching of chin but no words.

* * *

The journey to Grandad's was really cool. The flight, the Heathrow Express train – whizzz! – and then the Tube – down all those stairs and then the tube appears like a monster out of the tunnel and whizzes you off through more tunnels. We stayed in Grandad's house. I had to share a room with ET but he was on Planet Zark most of the time anyway.

Grandad seemed very quiet but he put on a big smile,

ruffled my hair and said, "Well, Becky, are you still mad about the football?"

Before I could answer, Mum shouted from the kitchen – "She's in the school team squad, I'll have you know. I told her it was in the blood!"

"It's only the under-ten squad, Mum."

"Well, that's good, that's good!" Grandad said. "You'll have to tell me all about that!"

So I did – about Mr O'Sullivan and big Simon and happy Goodwill and training on Wednesdays and my solo runs – and everything.

"I'm very impressed, Becky." Grandad seemed really proud of me. "You know what? You and me are going down to the park later and you can show me your skills. And maybe I can teach you one or two tricks!"

The man who had played in Croke Park was going to teach me football tricks. Brill!

First we had to visit Granny in the hospital. I don't like hospitals much. Don't like the smells. And the tubes going into people. I hadn't seen Granny since she came over for my First Communion. I got quite a shock. She was so thin and her voice was just a whisper.

"And how is my little Rebecca?" She took my hand in hers. I could feel every bone in her hand.

A Big Surprise

"I'm fine, Granny." She held on to my hand and gave a sort of smile. I could see Mum dabbing her eyes on the other side of the bed.

Dad took ET and me away while Mum and Grandad stayed on with Granny.

"Is Granny going to die?" I asked Dad as we travelled on a big red London bus.

"She's not very well, Becky. Not well at all. You'll have to say a little prayer."

We went on the London Eye – a great big wheel that takes you SO high. You can see all across the city. I had never been up so high before. It was amazing. But as we came slowly down I kept thinking of Granny's hand and how I could feel every bone in it.

9

Grandad

Later that day, we met up with Grandad. Mum stayed on in the hospital with Granny.

"Right," Dad said, checking his watch. "Next stop – 'The Future is Now' – an amazing exhibition in Earl's Court."

ET's eyes lit up.

"Would you like to come, Grandad?"

Grandad had gone very quiet again.

"Ah, no. I think I'll give it a miss. I'm not too bothered about the future just now, so if you don't mind –"

"Grandad and I have a date in the park," I blurted out suddenly. When I said it, I couldn't believe I'd said it.

"But Becky . . ." Dad was taken aback. "This is all

about your future, the world you're going to grow up in . . ."

"It's all right, Becky. You go with your Dad," Grandad said.

"No, I WANT to go to the park with you, Grandad. New tricks – remember?"

Grandad smiled. It was settled. As far as I was concerned my future was *now*, in the park with Grandad.

We sat on a bench in the park watching squirrels scuttling across the grass and up and down trees.

"Them boys can run, Becky. Look at them! If you could run like them no-one would catch you on the pitch, would they?"

"No way. Tell me about playing in Croke Park, Grandad."

"Oh now, who has been telling stories! That was a long time ago – over fifty years. I was only seventeen, playing for Meath minors in the Leinster Championship Final. And Croke Park was nothing like it is today. But it was wonderful – to go out and play where my heroes played – Peter McDermott and Frankie Byrne. I loved every minute of it. I wished it would go on forever. And I scored two points. The only problem was – WE LOST! But sure, that's the way of the world, Becky. That's the way of the world."

"But did you never play there again?"

"No. Got a pile of injuries and was out of action for a few years and then . . ."

"And then?"

"And then I met . . . and then I met . . . your Granny . . ."

"And then?"

"Oh but you are the curious one, Becky! And then the problem was a job! It was very hard to get a job then – so Granny and I got married and went off to London. Drove a bus for forty years – and here I am!"

"You drove a bus for forty years and you played in Croke Park! Cool! My dream is to play in Croke Park – and maybe drive a bus too!"

"Well, you just hold on to your dreams, Becky. You never know!"

Grandad reached into a shopping bag. "Now, that's enough talk. Time for some action!"

He took out a beautiful football. Not plastic. Real leather.

"I got this for you earlier. Now let's see some Shannon style."

"I hope Mrs Pratt never gets her hands on this ball," I said, tipping it from toe to hand.

"Mrs Pratt?"

Grandad

. I told him about our neighbour and her hydrangeas and her savage dog.

"Well, Becky, if you learn how to control and kick the ball properly, Mrs Pratt will never even get a smell of it," Grandad laughed.

"I hope not. It does smell lovely and leathery."

For the next twenty minutes we played serious stuff. Grandad went in goals (two coats) and I took shots. We practised hand-passes, foot-passes, hitting the ball with the outside of the foot, blocking a kick, hitting a target (a huge elm tree) – and solo runs, except that I didn't need to practise them. Even with ordinary shoes I amazed Grandad with my solo runs.

"You're teaching me now, Becky, for sure. Where did you learn to solo like that?" he gasped.

"Don't know. I just sort of taught myself. Mum says it's in the blood."

"Maybe she's right, but I could never solo like that! Do it again!"

I did. Again. And again. And again.

"Brilliant!" Grandad said. "Now I have only one more trick to show you – the shimmy!"

"The sh-shimmy?"

"The shimmy. Now watch me. I'm a forward coming in with the ball. You're a back. Try to stop me!"

45

Some chance, I thought – with the size of him and the size of me – but I moved forward to try and get the ball.

Suddenly he was gone the other way, right past me.

"How did you do that?" I gasped.

"That was the shimmy! Watch again!"

He showed the ball and then did a little trick with his feet, like a step we do in Irish dancing. Then he was gone the other way.

"One more time! Watch closely now!"

He did the shimmy again. It seemed easy when he did it. He handed me the ball. "Now it's your turn!"

Of course I tripped and fell in a heap (like Simon) the first time I tried it.

"Don't worry! Try again!" He didn't even laugh.

I tried again. At least I didn't fall this time. I kept trying. All the time Grandad kept praising me.

"You have it now . . . That's nice . . . Try another one . . ."

And then, I could do it – almost like him.

"Good girl! There'll be no stopping you now! Do you know what they used to call me when I was a young fellow, Becky?"

"The Shimmy?" I guessed.

"Nearly right," he laughed. "I was called 'Jimmy the Shimmy'! Jimmy Shannon – 'Jimmy the Shimmy'.

Many's the fellow I made a fool of with the shimmy.
Maybe they'll call you 'Becky the Shimmy' now!"

It didn't sound as good as 'Jimmy the Shimmy'.

Grandad looked at his watch. "Time to go, Becky.
We have to meet your Mum."

We walked back to the hospital. Grandad took my
hand and we skipped along, playing a game of "Don't
Walk on the Lines"! Grandad laughed as I tried to
avoid the lines on the path. Just when it seemed I
could not avoid a line, I had a brilliant idea. I did a
shimmy and danced over the line.

"Ah brilliant, Becky, brilliant! You're a star!" He
ruffled my hair. "Do you know what I'm going to tell
you?"

"Hardly, Grandad!"

"I don't know when I had such fun. And you took
my mind off . . . You took my mind off – things. God
bless you, child."

He squeezed my hand until it hurt, but I didn't
mind. We had reached the hospital. I knew what he
was thinking about: Granny.

Mum was waiting for us. She looked sad and her eyes
were red.

"I thought you two had forgotten about me," she
said, almost in a whisper.

"Becky and me had some important business in the park," Grandad explained, giving me a big wink.

Mum looked down at my feet. "Becky, look at the state of your shoes! What on earth were you up to?"

"It's only a bit of muck. Clean muck!" Grandad explained.

"I can do the shimmy, Mum. 'Jimmy the Shimmy' showed me!"

She looked at me and then at Grandad. "Honestly! I don't know which of you is worse!" she sighed as she searched in her handbag for a tissue to clean my shoes. At least she was smiling now.

10

Dreaming

On the flight home from London Mum was very quiet. Dad and ET were still excited about "The Future is Now". ET. had some new gizmo to play with. He offered me a go, but I wasn't interested. He probably just wanted to show off anyway. As far as I was concerned The Future was The Shimmy. All the way home I was doing the shimmy in my head.

I thought a lot about Grandad too. He was very lonely when we were leaving. I remembered his words – "Hold on to your dreams, Becky." I think that is good advice, because I'm always dreaming – scoring the winning goal, doing the shimmy, playing in Croke Park. If I put them all together that would be the BIG DREAM. That dream would last the whole flight home . . .

"And welcome back to Croke Park for the final moments of the Ladies All-Ireland Senior Football Final . . . Down in the corner little Becky Buckley – or Becky Bucks as she is known – is one angry woman. Her team are two points down with only minutes to go and I think she is angry with her teammates because they are not getting the ball down to her. She's walking round in circles, shaking her head, muttering to herself and now and then shouting to her teammates upfield . . ."

"Becky, are you all right?" Mum had spoken at last.
"Of course I am. Why?"
"You just look very . . . very cross."
"No. I was just dream– eh, thinking about stuff."
"Well, it must be very serious stuff!"
Gee, thanks, Mum. Now where was I?

"I see Becky is taking off her glasses and wiping them with her jersey. She was telling me earlier that when she was little her mum told her that the glasses were only 'corrective' and she wouldn't need them when she grew up. But Mums aren't always right and Becky still wears glasses, although they are special bendy ones, she tells me. Now what's she doing? She has run the length of the field, right up to her own goalmouth.

50

Dreaming

I think she has decided that if her mates cannot get the ball to her, she will go and get it herself! And now she has it! This is going to be interesting, folks! The crowd are loving it. Just listen to that roar – 'GO, BECKY, GO!' . . ."

" – go, Becky? Hey, Becky, I said do you want a go on my Super Interactive Digital Laser World War Three Game? It's your last chance!" It was ET.

"No I don't want a go on your silly super –"

"Becky! Your brother is only being kind and sharing!"

"Sorry. I was just – somewhere else!"

"You're *always* somewhere else, Becky."

"I said I was sorry. I just don't feel like playing his game just now. That's all."

"Well there are proper ways of saying that."

It was Mum who had the cross face now.

ET pulled a face and slid back into his seat.

Now, where WAS I?

"Yes, here we go folks! Becky is off on one of her famous solo runs. 'Go, Becky, go!' the crowd roars. She's gone past one opponent, past two. This is magical stuff. But now she faces Mary Jo Joyce who

51

is not easily passed. Oh, did you see THAT? Becky just did the perfect shimmy and left Mary Jo sprawling! She's only forty metres out. Can she go all the way and win this game in the last minute? The full-back is coming to tackle her. Another shimmy! Brilliant! She's clear on goal. A powerful shot with the outside of the boot. Right-hand corner of the net. G-O-O-O-O-A-L! She's done it! Becky Bucks has won the match with the very last kick of the game. Unbelievable!"

" – unbelievable! You really are, Becky! The hostess has been waiting for ages for you to fasten your seatbelt. We're about to land in Dublin. Here, let me do it."

"It's all right, Mum. I can manage."

"Hmmph! I wonder . . ."

She might at least have waited until I was presented with the Cup and the Woman of the Match award . . .

11

Something Spectacular!

For once, I couldn't wait to go back to school. Not to tell Miss Lane about my BIG DREAM, of course. I know what she would say – "Dreaming is for bedtime, Becky." Boreen. No, I wanted to get back to squad training to show Mr O'Sullivan my shimmy. I showed it to Josh. He thought it was cool, especially when he found he couldn't do it very well himself.

"It's a gift," I explained. "It's in the blood."

"In the blood?"

I told him about Grandad – 'Jimmy the Shimmy'.

"That's awesome!" Josh said. That's another one of his words. Awesome!

However, before school re-opened, there was another BIG SCENE at home. You've guessed it. Shona.

"Didn't you go to Mogsy's gig?" Mum enquired.

"Of course I did."

"And?"

"And nothing."

"What do you mean nothing?"

"He completely IGNORED me."

"Mogsy?"

"Of course. After all I did for him. I supported him when he was nobody."

"I would have thought he still is!" Dad suggested. Shona ignored him.

"I sent his demo tapes all over Dublin. I got him the gig. I am The Forever Undead's manager after all. Or at least I WAS until Saffron McGillicuddy came along. Purring like a cat, following Mogsy everywhere. And he just IGNORED me. ME, his manager. I couldn't believe it. I hate Saffron McGillicuddy. I hate Mogsy. I hate The Forever Undead. I hate EVERYTHING. I am SO depressed. I'm never going outside again –"

"To school?"

"To anywhere. You don't understand. My life is OVER, OVER."

She threw her Forever Undead tape in the bin and ran upstairs to her room, sobbing loudly. I hope I never have trouble like that with boys.

Shona stayed in her room all weekend. Mum

brought her some nice food but she only picked at it.

"Isn't love a terrible thing all the same?" said Dad, as he carried yet another tray of goodies down the stairs.

"Isn't it?" said Mum, standing on his toe as she took the tray.

"OUCH!"

Why is she always standing on his toe? I'll never understand grown-ups. Anyway you'll be pleased to know that I found a good home for the goodies – in my tummy.

Shona was finally persuaded to go back to school when it re-opened on the Monday. Off she went in her Ray-Ban glasses – in November! – looking like Jennifer Aniston hiding from press reporters. Luckily, for all of us, Saffron McGillicuddy goes to a different school.

First day back. Of course Miss Lane would make us write a story about "My Mid-Term Break". Boreen. So I wrote about flying to London (on a plane, not by just flapping my arms. That was a joke. Miss Lane didn't think it was funny), visiting my sick granny, going on the London Eye and playing with my grandad in the park. "And then we came home. It was fun."

The usual stuff. I didn't say anything about the shimmy because that would be my big surprise at training on Wednesday. I thought Wednesday would never come but, sure enough, it did.

* * *

The shimmy was a great success. It was a big surprise for Mr O'Sullivan, for everyone, but especially for Simon. Simon was in one of his worst tempers ever. Mr Long had called him into his office that day to ask if he knew how Goodwill's schoolbag got up on the roof of the school. Of course Simon said he didn't know. Of course we all knew how it got there but no-one actually saw Simon do it. So, Simon was in a temper, not just a temper but one of his worst tempers ever. He was charging around like a mad bull, even when the ball was nowhere near him. Mr O'Sullivan warned him that he would get a red card if he did not calm down.

I had a narrow escape. The mad bull charged past me and knocked me off balance. I tumbled to the ground just beside a big tuft of grass. I lay there for a moment. There was a very strong and nasty smell coming from the tuft. I peered in with my bendy plastic glasses.

It was a HUGE cow dung. Enormous. The cows had been in The Paddocks during the mid-term break and this cow had spent a long time at the toilet. A very long time. That's what I mean about a narrow escape for me. I had a wonderful idea. If it worked, it would be SPECTACULAR.

I stayed quite close to the smelly tuft.

"Are you all right, Becky?" Mr O'Sullivan enquired.

"Just getting my breath back."

"Okay. Take your time. We'll have to put a chain on this Simon fellow."

I waited and waited. Then my chance came. The ball came to me. I soloed around for a few seconds. Out of the corner of my eye, I could see Simon coming like a train, as I thought he would.

"My ball, Specky Becky!" he roared.

He lunged forward, arms outstretched.

Then I did it. My shimmy.

It was perfect. In a flash I was gone the other way, but there was no stopping Simon. He did a lovely swallow-dive and then crash-landed into the smelly tuft. It really was SPECTACULAR!!!

OWWW! ARRGH! SPLATTER! YEUCH!

The cow dung (nice and fresh and SOFT) sprayed in all directions.

Everybody froze. Simon finally skidded to a halt. He lay still for a moment, then slowly picked himself up.

He was covered in the brown stuff from head to toe. His hair was plastered with it. His face was like the mudpack that Mum sometimes puts on – except that it was a different kind of mud. The dung ran down his arms and legs. His jersey and shorts were soaked with the stuff. SPECTACULAR!!!

He combed the stuff out of his eyes and spat it out of his mouth. He looked down at himself in amazement.

"*MAAA-MEEE!*" he bawled and he ran for his life out the gate and down the road to his home.

Slowly the rest of us came to life again. Mr O'Sullivan tried to blow his whistle but instead he nearly swallowed it. He waved his arms furiously. At first I thought he was choking, but then I realised he was laughing.

"I . . . think . . . that'll do . . . for today, lads."

Now everyone was laughing. I was more kind of smiling. I was just pleased that my plan had worked with such SPECTACULAR results.

"Becky Bucks! Come here to me." Mr O'Sullivan was still heaving with laughter. "Where on earth did you learn that trick?"

"Oh it's just something I picked up in London," I said, trying to act real cool.

"In London?"

Something Spectacular!

I told him about Grandad, also known as 'Jimmy the Shimmy'.

"Well, he certainly taught you well, Becky. That was sheer class. And you certainly taught Simon a lesson. MAAA-MEEE will have him under the shower for the next hour! That was the best laugh I've had in ages. Now, is everybody here?"

Everybody wasn't here. Goodwill was still at the scene of the crime, pretending to do swallow-dives and laughing his head off.

"Goodwill! Goodwill! Come on, boy! We're going."

Goodwill jogged up to join us, shaking his head and laughing all the way.

"Man, that was the FUNNIEST thing I have ever seen! You're real cool, Becky."

12

Silent Simon

To be honest, I wasn't feeling too cool on my way to school the next morning. I was terrified of meeting Simon. I could already hear Mr Long's voice coming over the radio.

"ATTENTION PLEASE! One of the toilets in Room 6 is blocked. Room 6 may use the toilets in Room 5 if necessary. Anybody who may have seen Rebecca Buckley being pushed into the toilet in Room 6 please report to the office. Thank you."

When I told Josh what had happened to Simon he had only one word to say – "Awesome!"

When we lined up in the yard next morning I looked

nervously around but there was no sign of Simon. Oh no, he's going to come in late with his huge dad and probably MAAA-MEEE. But no – Simon never turned up.

Goodwill was still laughing. Goodwill is always laughing. "Man, that Simon," he chuckled, "he's probably still under the shower!"

At lunchtime, Mr Long was on duty in the yard. He gave me a big wink and a sort of shimmy – not a very good one, I have to say. I was safe for another day.

Simon did come to school the next day but, amazingly, nothing happened. He had a big scowl on his face but he said nothing to me – or to anyone else – which is unusual for Simon. Even when Teacher asked him a question, he just sat there and scowled. Maybe it was the wrong question?

"Who can tell me three things we get from the cow? Simon?"

Scowl! Giggles all around. Miss Lane had obviously not heard the news.

"I don't see what's so funny about the question. Ciara?"

"Ehm . . . milk . . . ehm . . . ice-cream and ehm . . . ehm . . . butter, Miss."

More giggles.

"Not exactly what I had in mind, Ciara. Milk yes, but . . . James?"

"Milk, meat, leather and I believe they can also make glue from the hooves." James is the class swot.

"Excellent, James."

Then down at the back of the class Rory said a VERY rude word. The whole class exploded into laughter. Miss Lane MUST have heard it too but she pretended she had not.

"What was that, Rory? Have you got another answer?"

"No, Miss," Rory said, trying hard not to laugh. Just then the bell rang for lunch break. Lucky for Rory.

When lunch break was over and we lined up in the yard to march back into class, one of the big boys from sixth class made a big cow-sound. "MOOOOOO!" Everyone knew who it was aimed at but Simon only made a worse scowl and kept his head down. Poor Simon! I actually felt sorry for him.

The other BIG news is that Shona is back with Mogsy and The Forever Undead. It seems that Saffron McGillicuddy made three BIG mistakes.

1. She spilled coffee into Mogsy's mixing machine (whatever that is – it's for making his recordings,

Shona says) and it cost him three hundred euro to replace it.

2. Mogsy discovered that Saffron has all of Orange Pimple's recordings. Mogsy HATES Orange Pimple (although with his spots, Mogsy should *be* in Orange Pimple . . .). Bad move, Saffron.

3. Mogsy discovered that Saffron is dating a French boy who is here to learn English. Mogsy HATES French boys. Worse move, Saffron.

So Saffron is gone and Shona is back. The dark glasses are gone. The doors don't bang any more. The Forever Undead are the greatest band ever – or will be when Shona does her Junior Cert and becomes full-time manager.

Dad is happy. He hates moods. Mum is not so sure. Mum is not in good form anyway. She's on the phone to Grandad every day about Granny.

Unfortunately Shona's tape of The Forever Undead is gone (yesterday was bin-day) but Mogsy is making her another one with his new mixing machine. (It's all right – Shona doesn't drink coffee. She says it would ruin her perfect skin).

Shona was really depressed about her "MOGSY 1" jersey. It went in the bin too. BUT as it happened Mum retrieved it and put it in Puddles' bed. A quick wash to get rid of Puddle-hairs and Puddle-smells and everything was perfect again. Shona was happy.

Too happy. She was full of her "Josh and Becks" jokes. And she pinched my Googlibar – my FAVOURITE bar.

"That's for eating all my goodies when I was . . . depressed," she explained.

"But you didn't WANT them!"

"Yes, because I was depressed – DOH! – and you should have been depressed for me too."

I never want to be a teenager. NEVER.

As I said, Shona getting back with Mogsy was the big news of the week. I'm not sure if it was the *best* news, though. Not for me, anyway.

13

The Writer

"Now children, I have a special treat for you today."

When Miss Lane makes an announcement like that, we all hold our breath. Will it be (another) Surprise Spelling Competition? Or (another) Sponsored Skipathon? Or (another) Cake Sale – ". . . and we'd like your parents . . ." – Mum will LOVE that. Another fifty Rice Crispie buns.

"We're having a special visitor."

Well, that at least was different.

"A writer! We have a writer coming to talk to us – for a whole hour. Isn't that exciting?"

Wow! No Maths class and no Irish Reading. This WAS exciting.

Actually The Writer was cool – and interesting. He

told us how we could all be writers. I don't want to be a writer. I want to be a footballer, but still . . .

"Now I'm sure you noticed something when I walked in. Miss Lane tells me you are all very bright – so you noticed that I am actually ALIVE! You noticed that, didn't you? The reason I say that is – when I was your age, which is only about four thousand years ago (Ha! Ha! Ha!) writers all had one thing in common – they were all very, very DEAD! It's true. They all lived long ago and far away. But now, here you have a real live writer in your classroom! And look – I don't have two heads or springy-sprongy things coming out of my one head (Ha! Ha! Ha!). I'm just an ordinary human being – an amazingly handsome one of course (Ha! Ha! Ha!). But that's the first thing about being a writer – you must be a human being. As far as I can see . . ." (he looked closely at us all) ". . . you are all humans. There are no aliens here!"

"What about Saul?" Rory whispered.

Giggles all around. Miss Lane frowned a HUGE frown and stood beside Rory for the rest of the talk.

"After that," The Writer continued, "you need to be FOUR things to be a writer. Only four! You need to be a sponge, a magpie, a cat and a daydreamer . . ."

More giggles. This was strange stuff. Miss Lane was frowning again.

The Writer

The Writer went on to explain what he meant. I think I remember most of it.

1. Being a SPONGE is about soaking things into your brain by *looking* – at people and places, reading books, watching television and all of that – and by *listening* – to your teacher (Miss Lane blushed), your parents, anyone who has a story, especially older people like Granny or Grandad (I thought of 'Jimmy the Shimmy') . . .

2. Being a MAGPIE is being a collector. (Only James knew that a magpie is a bird that collects shiny things). The Writer didn't want us to collect shiny things ("Ha! Ha! Ha!") – he wanted us to collect ideas, stories, information, words . . . Collect words? Yes, words, because words paint pictures and the more words we have, the better pictures we paint. That's what The Writer said.

3. Being a CAT means . . .

"Does anyone know what killed the cat?"

Rory guessed it was a dog. Ciara guessed a car.

But good old James had the answer. "I believe it was Curiosity."

"Good man," The Writer said. "Curiosity killed the cat – that's a very old saying, even older than me! (Ha! Ha! Ha!) – but listen to what it says. Curiosity is a

BAD thing! Rubbish! Curiosity is a GOOD thing. To be a writer you need to be curious about things, to be WONDERFUL like me! (Ha! Ha! Ha!). You need to be wonder-ful, full of wonder."

So far so interesting, but I have to say I was getting a bit tired at this stage. I was imagining myself scoring a super goal in training . . .

4. Being a DAYDREAMER is a good thing!
    (What? What's this?)
    "I know Teacher may give out to you for daydreaming" (she certainly does – 'Dreaming is for bedtime, Rebecca . . .') "- but it is actually a good thing to do . . ."

I stole a glance at Teacher. The HUGE frown was back.

"Of course," The Writer added quickly, "you can't be doing it all the time, but it's good to do because you are using the wonderful gift of –?"
    "Imagination," James piped up.
    "Exactly. Now I want you to daydream –"
    "That won't be a problem," Teacher said. "Most of them do it all the time!"

"Well, that's good," The Writer said. "I'm delighted to hear it."

Miss Lane frowned seriously and looked at her watch.

"I only want you to dream for twenty seconds. Just close your eyes and go wherever you want to go – now!"

More giggles, but we all tried hard.

Then . . .

"I was driving a tank," Rory said.

"Went home to bed," Simon grunted.

"Went to Los Angeles and met Brad Pitt and he fell in love with me . . ." (Yes, you guessed right. Ciara).

Saul made history by finding a ten-thousand-year-old worm in the Sahara desert.

Goodwill went to Nigeria to see his Granny.

And Becky Bucks scored the winning goal for her team in the Schools Cup Final in Croke Park – of course!

"Brilliant!" said The Writer. "Wonderful dreams. So dream and dream and dream and be a sponge and a magpie and a cat and you will all be writers. Thank you!"

We all clapped, especially when the bell for lunch break went just then. Miss Lane was shaking her head. She smiled as she said goodbye to The

Writer, but when he had gone the HUGE frown came back.

"Good evening and welcome to another edition of 'Sporting Heroes'. My special guest this evening is that brilliant footballer Becky Buckley who has just won her sixth All-Ireland medal in a row and was once again leading scorer in the Championship with an amazing eleven goals and thirty-six points and Player of the Year for 2022 . . ."

(APPLAUSE as Becky enters the television studio, wearing a slinky black dress to match her designer glasses . . .)

"Becky, before we talk about your sporting career, I'd like to talk about your family life. You live a lonely life now, don't you?"

"Yes, I suppose I do – but as long as I have football . . ."

"Of course, but tell us briefly what happened to your family. It IS an extraordinary story . . ."

"Well, briefly as I can . . . Mum and Dad separated when she became road manager for Robbie Williams. Dad went to California to do research and, I believe, married a rich widow who is funding his research. My

The Writer

brother claimed when he was fourteen that aliens from another planet were coming for him because they needed a superior brain. He walked out the door on Christmas Eve 2011 and we never saw him again . . ."

"Fascinating! And even your dog . . .?"

"Yes, poor old Puddles went next door to dig up his bone under the hydrangea bush and we never saw him again either, but I think I know what –"

"Well, time is moving on, Becky, but we must hear about your beloved older sister."

"Beloved? Oh yes, Shona. Beloved Shona was manager of the band The Forever Undead and she ran off with the lead singer Mogsy to a mountain in Tibet where they are devoting their lives to world peace through music."

"Amazing, you must miss them all so much, especially beloved Shona –"

"Becky! Are you in there?" Shona was thumping my bedroom door. "Josh is downstairs. Wants to know if you'll go down to the shops with him. Josh and Becks go on a shopping spree – truly awesome!"

Dreambuster! She should have stayed in Tibet. We would have *so* much more peace . . .

14

Disaster

I was still feeling nervous when we went to training on the Wednesday afternoon. I imagined Simon would wait and choose the moment to get revenge for the "Cow dung Incident," as Mr O'Sullivan called it. He would probably do a "Zinedine Zidane" on me – a head-butt which would put me in hospital for a week and finish my brilliant football career . . .

But nothing happened. Simon never came near me and never spoke a word. This was the new Silent Simon. Mr O'Sullivan put us through a skills session – catching, kicking, passing, blocking, soloing – and then he made us run forwards, backwards, zig-zag. I was exhausted and was glad when he called us together in the middle of the field.

"Now lads –" (*Don't forget Ciara and me, Mr*

O'Sullivan!), the time has come for some serious action —"

"Man," panted Goodwill, "what we just did was pretty serious."

"I'm talking about a game, Goodwill – a real game against a real team. We've done enough skills. The Primary Schools League starts in two weeks. That's the serious stuff, so we need a match to find out how good – or bad – we are. I have arranged a challenge match with St Mark's for Saturday morning in the Park. Now they are good, seriously good. They won the Under-Ten Championship last year and their coach tells me most of them are still under ten this year. I think they started playing when they were in nappies!"

"They probably still are in nappies – gross!" said Rory.

We all laughed – a bit nervously.

"I hope you're as sharp in the goals on Saturday, Rory. These fellows will be coming at you from all sides. Anyway this will be a good test and I want the whole squad to turn up. Everyone will get a chance. So just give it your best shot. Now let's do our huddle!"

We formed a circle and put our arms round each other's shoulders. Unfortunately I ended up between Rory and Simon. Apart from the fact that I couldn't even reach Simon's shoulders, I felt nervous being this close to him. Would this be the moment of revenge? I took a big breath and joined in.

"Who are the greatest?" Mr O'Sullivan barked.

"Ballybawn!" we chanted.

"Didn't hear you."

"BALLYBAWN!" we roared.

"Who will win on Saturday?"

"BALLYBAWN!" (actually Rory whispered "St Mark's").

"What do we say?"

"Go, Ballybawn, Go!"

We gave each other "high fives". My hand was stinging for a while after Simon's "high five". I don't think Simon knows how strong he is. Or maybe he does.

* * *

D – I – S – A – S – T – E – R! That's the only word for it. St Mark's – six goals and four points; Ballybawn – one goal. Disaster. Yes, St Mark's were good. They were brilliant, but we were awful. Nothing went right for us. We did everything wrong – passed when there was no-one there, didn't pass when there was – lost possession too easily – didn't seem to know where the goals were – or where the St Mark's players were. And when I say "we" I mean "we." I was as bad as everyone else. Went on a solo run and lost the ball. Did a shimmy and it worked. Did another and it didn't. There seemed to be three of them for every one of us. Mr O'Sullivan took me off in the second half. I was kind of glad he did. Simon scored our goal by just barging his way through and while Rory made some good saves, there were no nappy-jokes as he picked the ball out of the net six times. For once Goodwill wasn't laughing. He was scratching his head most of the time. Disaster!

That's how Mr O'Sullivan saw it too.

"A total disaster, lads. A total disaster. No other words for it. I told ye they were good and they *were*. But what were we at, lads? We made it easy for them. We did some nice things but we did them on our own. We didn't play at all AS A TEAM. Didn't look up to see who could use the ball, to see who was better placed. This is a team game, lads. A team game. If we don't get that into our heads, there will be no point in turning up against Holy Angels in a couple of weeks' time. So I hope we have learned a lesson here today." He paused, glaring around. "What have we learned, lads?"

"A lesson."

"What kind of game is it, lads?"

"A team game."

"Didn't hear you!"

"A TEAM GAME!"

I walked home depressed. Josh was tricking around with a ball in his garden.

"Hey, Becky. Wanna play?"

"Not just now, Josh."

Right now, Croke Park seemed a million zillion miles away.

15

Granny

The telephone woke all of us at six o'clock in the morning. Mum dashed downstairs. There was silence for a few moments. Then Mum began to sob loudly. Granny was dead. I suddenly remembered holding her hand and being able to feel all the bones. Ours was a quiet house that morning, except for Mum sobbing. Dad kept saying, "It's for the best, love. It's for the best."

Shona asked if we had to go to school and Dad said of course we had to. Nice try, Shona.

There was a photograph on the mantelpiece of Granny holding me as a baby in her arms. She was smiling and her hands were pudgy, not bony. "This is my darling Rebecca," I could hear her say, "though I would much prefer Marguerita . . ." Without thinking, I slid the photograph into my schoolbag.

I told Miss Lane my news and showed her the photograph. She was very kind and put her arm around my shoulders. She told the class and we all said prayers for Granny Shannon in heaven. Teacher propped the photograph on her desk so all day long Granny was smiling away at all of us. It was a nice feeling. Teacher said I was the only one in the class who had a granny in heaven, so I was special. I would prefer to have her in London but I suppose I am special. Teacher can be cool, sometimes.

On the way home from school I thought a lot about Grandad. He would be very lonely now without Granny. He had told me that next year they would be fifty years married and he was going to give her a big surprise. He would take her on a luxury cruise in a big ship to South Africa, but it was a SECRET and I must not tell anyone . . . And I didn't. Poor Grandad.

Mum seemed to spend the next week on the telephone – talking to Grandad and Aunt Rita and organising Granny's funeral. In the end Mum and Dad decided they would go to the funeral on their own.

"And what about us?" Shona whinged.

"You are big boys and girls," Dad said. "We'll

leave you a loaf of bread and a few tins of beans. You'll be fine! Only joking!" he added quickly.

"It will only be for two nights," Mum said softly. "It's all arranged. Shona will stay with the Brennans and Josh's mum has agreed to take ET and Becky. And you must all be very good while –"

"But I wanted to say goodbye to Granny," Shona wailed, which only started Mum crying again.

"It's all arranged," Dad said firmly.

Maybe Shona did want to say goodbye but I think she really wanted to see London too. At least she would have her beloved Mogsy to comfort her.

* * *

Staying in Josh's house for two nights would be cool – or so it seemed until I discovered I would have to share a room with Storm. Not cool.

"Don't put your stuff in my wardrobe – there isn't room."

"You can look at my dolls but you can't play with them – they're special."

"And that's my private bathroom – you can use the other one outside."

It was like a film star's room. On every wall there were photographs – of Storm.

Storm – just one day old. Storm – at one month.

Storm with her first tooth. Storm's first birthday party (with half the town of Chattanooga in the background). Storm. Storm. Storm.

"Are you sure it's all right for me to sleep in this bed, Storm?"

"I suppose so. As long as Mum didn't put my Britney Spears sheets on it, it's okay, I guess."

Yeuch! If there were Britney Spears sheets on the bed I would gladly have slept on the floor.

We had strange things like pancakes and syrup for breakfast and corn on the cob and meatloaf for dinner. And I'm not sure what was in my school sandwich but there was one happy crow who seemed to enjoy it behind the shelter in the school yard. Josh's Mum and Dad (I can't believe they are Storm's Mum and Dad too) were very kind to us, but I was really looking forward to our own mum and dad coming home. ET was fine – he had serious talks with Josh's dad about space exploration. Josh and I played soccerball until it was dark – and then Storm took over . . .

"I don't want to watch that DVD – it's so boring."

"Well, why don't you watch television in your own room and we can watch this DVD?"

"NO. I want a different DVD."

Et cetera. Et cetera. Et cetera.

For once I didn't mind going to bed early, although

going to sleep was not easy. Storm was in and out to her private bathroom trying on and taking off make-up.

"Do you think this suits my eyes? You wouldn't know, I guess . . ."

No. Storm, I wouldn't know and I wouldn't care. Just go to bed, please. When she did climb into bed, having said goodnight to each of her thirty-four dolls, someone started playing rock music very loudly down the road. It almost seemed as if it were coming from our house, but it couldn't be. Please, Mum and Dad, don't miss your flight. Zzzz . . .

* * *

"I hope you were all very good for the last two days," Mum said as we all sat down to tea (no corn on the cob!) next evening.

"Yes, Mum. Now tell us about the funeral –"

There was a loud knock on the front door. Dad went to answer it. There was a very angry voice outside. I thought it sounded like Mrs Pratt. It couldn't be. Mrs Pratt *never* comes to our door – but it was her.

I heard Dad invite her into the sitting room and then call Mum. The door was closed and we waited . . . Two minutes later, another angry voice. This time it was Dad.

"Shona! Come in here – AT ONCE!"

Here's what happened – in a nutshell.

The Brennans' baby became very ill the previous night and the parents rushed it to hospital. Shona got on her mobile to Mogsy who arrived up to our house with his drummer, Jazz. Shona let them in and they had a long practice session until well after midnight. (So I *was* right – the music did come from our house). Result – Mr and Mrs Pratt got hardly any sleep. Nor did poor Scotty. They were just about to ring the guards when the music stopped and Shona snuck back to the Brennans' house.

Dad was furious. Even with the doors closed, ET and I could hear him tearing strips off poor Shona.

". . . total lack of trust . . . very disappointed in you . . . no thought for your neighbours . . . apologise to Mrs Pratt AT ONCE . . . you are grounded for a week, Madam . . . understood?"

Ours was a very quiet house for the next day until Mum gave a shriek the following afternoon.

"Shona! Come here AT ONCE!"

Mum had found two beer cans under the sofa and a beer stain on her beautiful beige carpet.

Shona is now grounded for two weeks.

Late News: Baby Brennan is home from hospital and is fine. Shona is totally depressed again and is not at all fine.

16

Holy Angels

Holy Angels they were NOT! I am talking about the first round of the Primary Schools League. I am talking about Ballybawn Primary School versus Holy Angels Primary School. Whoever gave it that name was SO wrong.

Most of the "Angels" were sneaky – pushing and pulling when they could get away with it. They complained to the referee non-stop.

"Ah, referee did you see THAT?"

"I never even TOUCHED him, referee!"

They dived – they would have been great in a swimming pool. They rolled over and howled with pain if anyone even brushed against them. Mr O'Sullivan said at half-time that they had been watching too much of the World Cup.

Oh by the way, I forgot to say – we won by four goals and three points to two goals and two points. WE WON!

Go Ballybawn, go!

And I scored a goal and a point! The goal wasn't much. I just sort of toe-poked it in from about two metres (despite their *enormous* full-back roaring "Out of the way, Specky!" at me) but – as Mr O'Sullivan said – it's all about being in the right place at the right time . . .

But the point – that was magic. Sheer class, Mr O'Sullivan said. I caught the ball out on the left wing, did a little solo run and looked up. There was no-one free to take the ball, so I decided I would have a go myself. The full-back charged at me but a lovely shimmy sorted him out . . . I took aim and hit the ball as high and as hard as I could, allowing for the wind, of course. I had worked all this out. It was going wide but at the last moment it curled in and floated over the bar. Mr O'Sullivan was right. Sheer class.

The best thing about it was that Mum was there to cheer me on. Cool! So was Shona – except that she didn't cheer at all. She scowled and complained that she was freezing and this was totally boring. She had no choice in the matter. Mum brought her along. It was part of being grounded.

Holy Angels

As I said, most of the Holy Angels were anything but angels. A few of them were all right. Luckily for me, Fiona was one of them. Fiona was my marker. She told me she was only on the team because Thomas hurt his big toe. From the way she described Thomas, I was sorry for his big toe but glad it kept him out of the match. Whenever the play moved to the other end of the pitch we had a little chat about our schools and teachers and stuff like that. I told her about Miss Lane being called Boreen. She thought that was very funny.

"Our teacher is Mr Short. We call him Fada. '*Fada*' – long – get it?"

I thought that was just as funny as Boreen. Suddenly a bark came from the sidelines as the ball came our way and I grabbed it.

"Ah, come on Fifi! You didn't come out here for a chat!" It was the Holy Angels' coach.

"I HATE being called Fifi," Fiona said later. "Makes me sound like a poodle. By the way, that's Fada," she added, pointing to the coach.

He was actually short – and round. He marched up and down the sideline, barking at his team and doing his share of complaining to the referee also. It became clear as the match went on that Fada and Mr O'Sullivan were not exactly best buddies. They were shouting and waving their arms at one another, especially when Simon got the ball.

Fada: "That fellow must be thirteen, if he's a day."

Mr O'Sullivan: "Do you want to see his birth certificate?"

At one point, the referee stopped the match and made the coaches go on opposite sidelines. Certainly, none of the Angels tried to be sneaky with Simon. I was glad we had Simon.

Goodwill was Man of the Match. He scored two great goals and laughed all the way through. I think the Angels thought he was laughing at them, but they couldn't know that Goodwill laughs all the time. At last the final whistle blew. WE WON! I said goodbye to Fiona. Fada and Mr O'Sullivan shook hands – sort of.

We got into our huddle.

"Well done, lads," Mr O'Sullivan said, rubbing his hands in delight. (*Well done, Ciara and me too, Mr O'Sullivan*). "Ye learned your lesson from St Marks. What kind of game is it, lads?"

"A TEAM GAME," we roared.

"A team game, lads. Proud of ye. Proud of ye – because ye were looking up, lads. What were ye doing?"

"Looking up."

"Didn't hear ye, lads!"

"LOOKING UP!" we shouted.

"That's it. Looking up for a better-placed player. Looking up. Team game. What are things doing, lads?"

We looked at each other.

"Looking up, lads. Things are looking up. What are things doing?"

"Looking up," we muttered.

"Didn't hear ye!"

"LOOKING UP," we bawled.

"That's it, lads. And what's the cry?"

"GO, BALLYBAWN, GO!" we cheered.

"Well done, lads. Proud of ye! Proud of ye!"

On the way home, Mum was beaming.

"I thought ye were brilliant. And my little Becksy-Wecksy was the most brilliant of all."

"I thought it was absolutely, totally and utterly BORING," snorted Shona.

I just lay back in the back seat and closed my eyes . . .

"SPORTS EXTRA! Special full-page report on the Ballybawn-Holy Angels clash –

A huge crowd was treated to a feast of football at

the Park Grounds when Ballybawn took on Holy Angels yesterday. It has to be said that most of the football came from the Ballybawn side who worked well as a team and were always LOOKING UP for a better-placed teammate. It has also to be said that the Holy Angels' tactics were to say the least doubtful. (Holy Angels they were NOT!)

Though not a big team – apart from their mighty midfielder Simon –Ballybawn were clever and classy. Man of the Match Goodwill scored two cracking goals but the player that took this reporter's eye was little Becky Bucks (pictured below on one of her solo runs) playing out on the wing. She scored a cheeky goal and a point that was worth going a long way to see. And as for her solo runs and shimmies – sheer class. Mark my words, you'll see Becky Bucks thrill the crowds in Croke Park in years to come. You read it first in SPORTS EXTRA!"

"Wake up, Becky," Mum called. "We're home!"

"Home, BORING home," grunted Shona.

17

The Rescue

I don't know how many times I have warned Josh not to kick the ball high when we're playing in Buckley Park – my home ground (Josh's home ground is the Chattanooga Superbowl). You know the reason why – it will usually mean another football for Mrs Pratt's collection. But if it's going to happen it's going to happen, I guess – as Josh would say.

It was a windy November evening. I *know* we shouldn't have been playing with Grandad's good football, but Josh likes playing with it. He dreams of becoming a kicker with the Dallas Cowboys some day and he likes to sky the ball. You already know what happened, I guess (I'm beginning to talk like Josh now). He skyed the ball up in the air. It screwed off his boot. The wind caught it and it floated right over the garden hedge. Josh–0, Mrs Pratt–1.

"Gee, I'm awful sorry, Becky. I kind of messed that one up, I guess."

"Kind of . . ." I muttered as I fell to my knees and tried to peer through the bottom of the hedge. I was really cross with Josh. I could see the ball sitting on top of the hydrangea bush. Disaster.

"I didn't mean to do it –"

"Shush!" I called, pulling him down out of sight. Mrs Pratt had come out to her garden, muttering. We sat very still. If she saw us we would get a lecture and no ball. The door of her garden shed opened and closed. We could hear her return to the house, still muttering to herself.

The back door banged. I peered into her garden again. Hydrangea bush with no ball.

"Thanks a lot, Josh," I said. "Thanks really a lot."

"Like I said, Becky – I didn't mean to –"

"I told you. I told you a hundred times not to kick it high, but you had to do your Dallas Cowboys bit!"

It seemed we were about to have our first big row.

"I said I was sorry. Anyway I gotta go. Mom will –"

"You're going nowhere until you help me get my ball back."

"Me? I ain't going in *there*. No way."

"Yes way. It's about time we struck back. That was my special football that Grandad gave me – and he's coming over for Christmas – and he's going to want to know where the ball is –"

"I'm not going in there."

"You kicked the ball in there."

"Not going. She would probably lock us in the shed forever."

"She won't see us. She will be in her front room. There's a hole in the hedge further up. We'll wait a little while until it's dark."

"I gotta go home. Mom will –"

"Chicken!"

"Am not!"

"Are so!"

"Am not!"

"We'll be in and out in two minutes. Chicken!"

"All right. Two minutes – that's it."

We waited until it got darker and then moved. We just about squeezed through the hole (made by Puddles – thank you, Puddles) and scurried across to the shed. This was exciting – like a break out from prison that you would see in the movies. Except that we were breaking *into* prison, to free the innocent footballs.

Thankfully the door wasn't locked but we had to

open it very carefully and quietly. It creaked noisily. We held our breath. No sign of life in the house.

"It wasn't very clever to wait until it's nearly dark," Josh whispered. "I can't see anything!"

"Just wait," I said.

Our eyes slowly got used to the half-light. There were pots everywhere – on shelves and on a table. An old-fashioned lawnmower, spades and forks, a wheelbarrow.

"This is useless," Josh whimpered. "I'm going –"

"No wait!" I cried. "Look over there – in the corner!" It was a barrel – almost full of footballs, with Grandad's ball right at the top.

"They're mine! They're all mine!" I felt like whooping with delight.

"Well, we can't bring them all. Hey, there's my American football!"

"Told you it would be worthwhile."

"Okay, okay. Let's just grab a few and go. This is spooky!"

As I stepped towards the barrel, I stubbed my toe on something. "OUCH!"

"Shush, Becky."

"It HURTS!"

I knelt down to feel what had tripped me. It was a latch – the latch of a trapdoor.

"Hey, Josh. This is interesting."

"This is spooky. Let's get the balls and go!"

But excitement and curiosity had got the better of me. My heart was pounding as I pulled up the trapdoor.

"No, Becky! No!" Josh pleaded. "You said two minutes."

"Maybe there are more footballs down here –"

"We have enough –"

"Or skeletons! Two more minutes – just to see what's down here. We'll never get the chance again."

"No way! I'm going –"

"Chicken!"

"Am not!"

"Are so! Look there's a torch fixed to the inside of the door. Isn't that clever?"

I switched the torch on, being careful to shine it down into the cellar. There was a ladder with eight steps down. I began the climb.

"You're crazy!" Josh snapped.

"Just curious!" I said with a nervous laugh.

Curiosity is a good thing. The Writer said that. I flashed the torch around. What it showed left both of us speechless.

18

Mrs Pratt's Secret

It was like a mini-supermarket down in the cellar. Shelf upon shelf of food – all tinned food. One whole shelf of tinned beans. Tinned fruit, tinned vegetables, tinned fish. Another shelf filled with packs of candles, boxes of matches and batteries. Two shelves packed with books. On the opposite side were bulky packages wrapped in heavy plastic. I shone the torch right up against the plastic. The packages were soft – blankets maybe and, yes, sleeping bags.

In the centre stood a table with a chess-set laid out and covered with plastic. Also a radio, wrapped in plastic.

Josh gave a low whistle.

"Awesome!" he whispered. "This is awesome. What is going on here?"

For once he was right. This *was* awesome – and very, very strange. I shone the light on the wall. There were photographs of people taken a long time ago – they must have been the parents of Mr and Mrs Pratt. There was a prayer of some sort in a frame:

> *Protect us, Lord*
> *When darkness comes . . .*

I couldn't read any more.

"I don't know what's going on but – YIKES! YIKES!"

The torchlight revealed two ghostlike heads hanging on the wall.

"They're murderers!" I gasped. "The Pratts. They've cut off the heads of –"

"No, silly." Josh took the torch and went right up to the ghostly heads. "These are gas-masks."

"GAS –masks?"

"Yes. They used them in the big World War way back. My dad collects books about the War. He's big into all this stuff. This is really awesome."

"Well, they sure scared me. Maybe we should go now. Our two minutes are up, Josh."

But now it was Josh who was full of curiosity.

"Don't you see, Becky? This is a bunker."

"A – bunker?"

"Yeh. It's where you hide if there's a war. Bombs and stuff falling."

"But there's no war!"

"Yeh. But the Pratts must be afraid of another big war. This is where they are going to hide and be safe. They have loads of food – and blankets. Books to read and candles for light. They could stay down here for ages. Awesome!"

Now the prayer made sense to me –

> *Protect us, Lord*
> *When darkness comes . . .*

"It's all too scary for me. Let's –"

THWACK! YIKES!

I had leaned against the bookshelves.

"What was that?" I was trembling now.

Josh peered in behind the books.

"It's just a mousetrap. You disturbed it –"

"A MOUSEtrap?"

"There's no mouse. You just –"

"Don't care. If there's a mousetrap, there's mice. Let's get out of here!"

Josh agreed this time. We climbed the steps back up to the shed.

THWACK-A-LACK! This was no mousetrap.

It was the shed door. A gust of wind had slammed it shut. We closed the trapdoor. I grabbed a couple of footballs and headed for the door.

"There's a problem," Josh said. "It's stuck. The door is stuck!"

"It can't be stuck!" I cried, but it was stuck fast.

We shoved as hard as we could but the door would not budge. The force of the wind had stuck it so fast that even our kicking it was no use. We were the mice caught in the trap. My heart was racing.

"What are we going to do? The Pratts probably heard the door slamming. They're going to catch us. And maybe murder us for discovering their secret . . ."

"Stay cool, Becky. They might not have heard the door. It's very windy outside."

"Well, we're still stuck in here. We could be here for ages . . ." I slumped to the floor and began to cry. "And it's all your fault. If you hadn't kicked the ball so high –"

"My fault? Whose idea was it to come in for the ball?"

"Yes but you –"

"And whose idea was it to go down the cellar?"

"Doesn't matter. We're going to die or –"

"No way. We have lots of food, if we can find a tin-opener . . ."

97

"Very funny."

I knew he was trying to be brave but I could see the fright in his face. We were doomed.

Josh wasn't giving up. He shone the torch around the shed.

"Maybe we can –"

"Shush, Josh!"

"What?"

"Shush! And put out the torch. There's someone outside!"

Sure enough, someone was tugging at the door-handle from the outside. This was it. Mrs Pratt. Probably with Mr Pratt, standing by with a brush. Or an axe. This was the end.

I couldn't breathe. Josh and I huddled together in the corner. More fiddling with the handle. A big tug and the door swung open. A pause. Then a voice spoke.

"Come on out, you pair of cats!"

A strange feeling came over me. I knew from the voice and slight figure standing in the gloom that it wasn't Mrs Pratt. It was Mogsy.

19

Safe!

"Mogsy! Am I glad to see you! But what are you doing here?"

"I could ask you the same thing, babe – but first let's rock and roll out of here."

I still had the torch in my hand. I turned to Josh.

"We'll have to put the torch back in the trapdoor, or else she'll know we were here!"

"She'll know anyway. Let's go!"

"Not before I get what I came for," I said, grabbing Grandad's football and another one for luck.

Josh took his American football.

Mogsy led the way through the hole in the hedge. He just about squeezed through.

"I have to tell you, babes, I tore my new leather

jacket carrying out this daring rescue. I just hope you're impressed by that."

I was very impressed and very thankful. I would never ever call our rescuer Spotsy again. I shivered when I thought of what might have happened if Mogsy had not come by, there and then. But what WAS he doing at the bottom of our garden on a dark winter evening?

"Simple. I came down to meet your big sis, who – as you know – is grounded, thanks to the Wicked Witch of the West." He nodded in the direction of the Pratts' house. "When I heard voices in the shed I thought it was her – the Wicked Witch. To tell the truth, when the wind slammed the door shut I was tempted to slip in and jam it shut – just to teach her a lesson – that nobody messes with Mogsy – but then I recognised your sweet little voice, babe, and I reckoned you were in some sort of trouble. So, Supermogsy to the rescue! Ain't you lucky, babe?"

I hated being called babe and, now that I knew Mrs Pratt's secret, I didn't like her being called the Wicked Witch either – but I was so thankful to Mogsy, I couldn't say anything to him.

"By the way, babe, what WERE you two doing in the witch's shed?"

We showed Mogsy the footballs and explained

how Mrs Pratt had been "collecting" them.

"Wow! Is she the Wickedest Witch or what? Now say 'thank you, Mogsy' and go and tell your big sis that Number One is waiting for her!"

"Th-thank you, Mogsy!" we stammered together and scuttled off through the shadows.

"I'd better go," Josh whispered, "or Mom will have a panic attack. See you tomorrow."

I passed the word to Shona who slipped out while Mum was on the phone. As for me – I flopped down on my bed and found myself shaking all over. I didn't know whether it was relief or fright or cold. I wrapped myself in the duvet and tried to make sense of all that had happened – Mrs Pratt's secret hideout, the terror of the jammed door and our rescue by – of all people – Mogsy.

"Wake up, Naughty Nora!" Shona was shaking me out of a deep sleep. "It's dinner-time, sleepyhead. Hey, whatever were Josh and Becks up to in the garden shed?" She gave me a big wink and skipped out of the room, laughing.

I bit my lip and followed her downstairs.

When Josh and I met up after school next day, neither of us knew what to say about our discovery of Mrs Pratt's secret. We were so relieved that Mogsy had come to our rescue, but we agreed that we would keep Mrs Pratt's secret. No-one else would be told of the secret room under the shed – the bunker, as Josh called it. I felt sorry for the Pratts. Why would they be so afraid of a war, here in Ireland? And I wondered, did the Pratts know we had discovered their secret?

The answer came in the following weeks. A "lost" ball suddenly re-appeared in our garden. In perfect condition. No "bite-marks" from Scotty. A week later another lost ball found its way into our garden. I said nothing. The Pratts were talking to me in their own way. "We know you know," they were saying. "We hope you will keep our secret." Whenever another ball went into the Pratts' garden – which was often enough, when Josh was around – it came straight back the same day. And there were no more complaints about hydrangeas being damaged.

20

A Stranger Calls

The Plum Puddings were our next opponents. Their proper name is Saints Peter and Paul National School. P and P – Plum Puddings – get it? They don't like being called the Plum Puddings. Of course they call us the Bully Boys (Ballybawn, B-B, don't bother getting it!). Bully BOYS! What about Ciara and me, you Puddings?

The Puddings' home ground isn't exactly Croke Park. For a start there's a slope in the pitch – a serious slope, which makes football hard work. And they don't bother cutting the grass too often, which makes football even harder work. We played against the slope in the first half. Most of the play was around our goals. We forwards didn't see much of the ball, but even so, I was exhausted by half-time. Just you try running up a hill of long grass a few times and you'll see.

In the quiet periods when the ball was in our goalmouth, I noticed a man on the sideline with Mr O'Sullivan. He was a stranger – definitely not one of the parents – but every now and then he would talk with Mr O'Sullivan.

"Who's that?" I called to Goodwill.

"Don't know!" Then a laugh. "Probably a Manchester United scout, sent over to watch ME!"

"Probably a guard, sent over to arrest some of you Bully Boys!" growled Goodwill's opponent.

Just to teach him a lesson, when the ball eventually came our way, Goodwill grabbed it and kicked over a point.

That was our only score of the half, but Mr O'Sullivan wasn't too worried at half-time. The Plum Puddings had only scored a goal and two points, thanks mainly to Rory's brilliant display in goal.

"Not to worry, lads. It's there for the winning. What is it, lads?"

"There for the winning," we muttered.

"Didn't hear you!"

"THERE FOR THE WINNING!" we roared.

"That's it. We have the skills and now we have the hill. I hope to see a lot more of you forwards in action.

A few more scores, Goodwill? And Becky – use that hill for your solo runs. Remember lads, we're Ballybawn. We're the best! What are we, lads?"

"WE'RE THE BEST!" we roared.

"That's the spirit, lads! Now go out and eat those Plum Puddings!"

We didn't exactly *eat* the Puddings, but it was really very easy with the hill. I got my solo runs working and I managed a few shimmies. One of the shimmies led to a goal, but Goodwill was the real star. He scored an amazing four goals and a point. Josh calls Goodwill our MVP – Most Valuable Player.

Final score – Ballybawn, five goals and two points. Plum Puddings, one goal and three points.

Mr O'Sullivan came around with a bowl of orange segments.

"Well done, lads. Proud of ye! Told ye we were the best!"

The stranger had followed our coach onto the pitch. He went around congratulating each one of us.

"This is a friend of mine, lads," Mr O'Sullivan explained. "He's from County Meath, but we'll forgive him that! His name is Seán Boylan and he was manager of the Meath team for about two hundred years, or so it seems." The stranger gave a hearty laugh. "He helped Meath win a few All-Irelands when we were taking a break down in Kerry. Anyway, he was kind enough to come along and see you in action today and he has a few words to say to you."

"You're a terrible man, Murty Sullivan," Seán Boylan began. Murty! What kind of a name was *that*?

"I won't keep you, lads – and lassies!" He bowed to Ciara and me. *(Thank you, Mr, Boylan. Were you listening, Murty?)*

Mr Boylan kept moving in and out among the Ballybawn players.

"The first thing is – enjoy your football. You play because you like the game – so enjoy it!

"Discipline is important too. There are rules in the game. Things you are allowed to do. Things you are not. The rules are there to protect you. So learn them – and keep them. If you make a mistake – do the wrong thing – don't worry about it. Learn from it. Next time you get a chance, you'll do the right thing.

"Also lads – and lassies – it's a team game. You play for the team, not for yourself. You play with the team, not by yourself. Sometimes you might not be picked on the team. Don't give out to poor Murty here! Just put your head down and try harder to get back on the team. Show Murty he was wrong!"

"I'm never wrong, Seán. You know that!" Mr O'Sullivan boasted.

"Last thing," Mr Boylan continued. "Football is a skilful game – so learn the skills. The catch, the pass, the tackle, the solo run, the pick-up. Practise them and practise them and practise them. As often as you can. At school, at home. All the time. Practise your skills. And talking of skills" – he suddenly turned to ME – "where did you learn to shimmy like that?"

I got such a shock that I couldn't speak. I shrugged my shoulders in embarrassment.

"It's a lovely skill – delightful to see in a youngster like you. It reminds me of a fellow long ago when I was your age. Jimmy Shannon. He was just brilliant with the shimmy. Do you know what they used to call him?"

"Was it 'Jimmy the Shimmy'?" I stammered.

"What?" Now it was Mr Boylan's turn to be shocked. "How did you know that?"

"He's my grandad." I wasn't embarrassed any more. I was proud, very proud.

"I don't believe it!" Mr Boylan turned to his friend. "Can you believe that, Murty?"

"It's a small world, Seán."

Mr Boylan turned back to me. "Where's your Grandad now?" he asked.

"In London – but he's coming to us for Christmas."

"Well, you tell him that we still remember 'Jimmy the Shimmy' down in Meath. And that no Kerryman could ever do the shimmy like him!"

Mr O'Sullivan ignored his friend's last remark. "Nearly time to go, lads."

"Any questions?" said Mr Boylan.

"Yeah," Goodwill said. "Are we good enough to win the Primary Schools Cup?"

"You could be," Mr Boylan said with a shrug of his shoulders. "I haven't seen the other teams – but I wouldn't get too worried about cups and medals. There will be plenty of time for that later. Just enjoy each game. Okay?"

We nodded, not too sure if Mr O'Sullivan would agree with his friend.

"Well, they're in the semifinal now," he said. "Only one step away from the big day out in Croke Park. Big *bualadh bos* for Mr Boylan, lads."

We clapped loudly for the stranger.

"Now off with ye and get changed before you catch your death of cold. Training on Wednesday. Practise your skills!"

Mr Boylan ruffled my hair as I ran past him.

"'Jimmy the Shimmy'! Imagine that!"

21

Croke Park Dreams

"One step away from Croke Park . . ." Mr O'Sullivan's words stayed in my head all weekend. One step away from my dream – to play in Croke Park. After training on Wednesday our coach gathered us together for a team talk.

"One step away from the final in Croke Park," he reminded us again. "But it's a big step. We face our old friends Saint Mark's in the semifinal."

"Our old enemies, you mean," Rory muttered.

"Whatever you like to call them," Mr O'Sullivan continued, "but they're good. Remember how they walloped us in a friendly match a while ago. But we're better now –"

"We're the BEST!" a voice piped from the back.

"Well said, Goodwill! And we'll have to stay the

BEST. So don't eat too much over Christmas, because we don't play Saint Mark's until the New Year."

"That's ages away," Ciara moaned.

"It won't be long coming round, Ciara. Just keep yourself fit. And just to find out what it will be like to get to the final, I have a little surprise for you – a special trip to Croke Park!"

There was a big cheer of approval.

"On Sunday week, Dublin play Kerry in a charity match in Croke Park. So I propose bringing the three teams – under-twelve, under-ten and under-eight – to the match. AND we'll take in a visit to the GAA Museum as well!"

Another big cheer.

"It will cost each of you the enormous sum of five euro – mainly to pay for the bus. So break open your piggy-bank and give your name to me if you want to go. And if you don't want to go, I'll want a good reason why!"

I thought Sunday week would never come. I was first up to Mr O'Sullivan with my name and my five euro. We were going to Croke Park! I had seen it often on television but – because no-one else in our house was really interested in Gaelic football – I never had the chance to go there. Now, thanks to our football coach, the chance was here. Good old Murty!

* * *

Josh sat beside me on the bus. We sang and cheered and waved and laughed all the way to Croke Park. Anyone seeing us would think we had just won the Sam Maguire Cup. Goodwill was in great form. He had made up a Ballybawn song to the tune of "Knick-Knack, Paddywhack":

BALLY-BAWN, BALLY-BAWN
We're the best you ever saw
With a Knick-Knack Paddywhack
Give a dog a bone
BALLY-BAWN
We're out on our own!

"Good man, Goodwill! You're a mighty man!" Mr O'Sullivan laughed.

We must have sung Goodwill's song two hundred times on the way to Croke Park.

The GAA Museum was our first stop. It was really cool. Films and videos of matches played long ago. Photographs of famous players and teams. Chances to try your skill (Simon nearly broke the sharp-shooting screen!). There was so much to see and do – we didn't have nearly enough time. I took one last look around . . .

"And here, ladies and gentlemen," said the guide in a hushed voice, "we have a very special item. Becky's

boots. Yes, we all remember Becky. Becky Buckley or Becky Bucks as her friends knew her. Winner of an amazing TEN All-Ireland medals IN A ROW before she retired in 2026 to spend the rest of her life as a doctor caring for the forgotten people of the Amazon jungle. In that last memorable final of 2026 she scored an AMAZING five goals and four points and, these ladies and gentlemen, (even more hushed voice) are the boots she wore that day. An AMAZING woman! Her heart may be in the Amazon jungle but her boots are still here in the GAA Museum in Croke Park – or Buckley Park as many call it nowadays –

"Becky Bucks, do you want to end up on display in the museum?" It was Mr O'Sullivan's booming voice. "Will you come on, girl? They are locking the place up!"

I dashed past him to join the others.

"Were you in a dream or what, girl?"

"No. It was a reality show!" I called back.

The match was cool too. Even though it was a December afternoon, dark with drizzle and mist – and even though it was only a charity match – it was played at a furious pace. The All-Ireland champions Kerry were stunned when Dublin scored two goals in the opening ten minutes. Kerry crept slowly back into the game and at half-time the sides were level. All of Ballybawn were screaming for Dublin, of course – along with about a thousand other children from Dublin schools. Poor old Mr O'Sullivan was almost a lone voice for Kerry in the middle of all the "Dubs", but that didn't stop him roaring his heart out for the "Kingdom" (that's Kerry) and telling the referee exactly what he thought of him . . .

"It's quite a ball-game, isn't it?" Josh said as he shared the enormous bucket of popcorn his mother had packed for him – along with his "survival kit" of a triple-padded Arctic anorak, giant woollen mittens and the craziest fur hat you ever saw.

"And quite a park," he added. "Awesome! Would you like a doughnut?"

Actually, I wasn't really tuned in to Josh and I did very little cheering either. I was just mesmerised by the game and the place. (I learned that word – mesmerised – from Shona who claims she was "mesmerised" the first time she heard Mogsy play the guitar. It means "under a spell"). I was kicking every ball. I was part of every move. I knew *exactly* why things went wrong. If *I* was there I would have done a shimmy here, a solo run there. I would have given that pass earlier and then cut inside to take the return . . . I would have drifted out to the wing to meet the ball coming out of our defence and then used my AMAZING speed to burst up along the sideline, before steadying myself to judge wind and rain before kicking an IMPOSSIBLE point right from under the stand . . . Oh yes, I could see it all, feel the spring of the grass under my boots, hear the roar of the crowd –

"Go Becky, go!"

"Bally-bawn! Bally-bawn – we're the best you ever saw . . ."

Oh yes, Croke Park was made for Becky Bucks and Becky Bucks was made for Croke Park. Out of the way, Saint Mark's. Here come THE CHAMPIONS!

22

Here Comes Sam!

Dublin won by two points. We teased Mr O'Sullivan all the way home on the bus, but he just laughed it off.

"Sure, that wasn't our real team at all. Just a crowd of boys we put out. Wasn't it a charity match, after all? We thought it would be a nice act of charity to let Dublin win because let's face it, they've won nothing for donkeys' years!"

We gave a big WOOOOOO!

"AND they had the referee on their side!"

We gave an even bigger WOOOOOO!

"Now," he continued, "ye had better be nice to me, because I have organised a big surprise for ye . . ."

Suddenly there was silence.

"I thought that might shut ye up! There's a very

115

special visitor coming to the school tomorrow. He's big and he's fat –"

"Must be Simon's dad," Rory whispered behind us.

"I know!" Goodwill roared. "It's Santa Claus!"

"Not quite, Goodwill." Mr O'Sullivan's eyes were sparkling now. "Even better than that. It's . . . Sam Maguire!"

"Ho – hum!" Ciara sighed.

"Can you believe it? The Sam Maguire Cup coming to Ballybawn! Only because I know the Kerry captain so well. He brought 'Sam' up for the Charity Match. I made a special request that he bring 'Sam' to Ballybawn and he said yes! He'll be in the school for a brief visit at eleven o'clock tomorrow. Tell your mums and dads they are welcome to come along. It will be the only chance to meet "Sam" because he lives permanently in Kerry now and forever more. Amen!"

Another WOOOOOO! for Murty.

When I mentioned the news at home, the reactions were as you might expect.

Dad – "Sorry. Business meeting in Galway."

Shona – "Is he a film star or something? A Cup? Who wants to see a Cup?"

ET – "Yeah, I'll be in the school but I have the computer booked for my project from eleven to twelve."

Mum – "Of course I'll be there!"

"Excuse me, Mum?"

"I'll be there. They don't understand, Becksy! (*Grrr!*) But we do – because football's in our blood!"

Mum never ceases to amaze me.

* * *

There was a near-riot in the school next day when "Sam" was paraded around the yard. Four hundred screaming children (correction – three hundred and ninety-eight –ET was on the computer and Saul was lost in his wormery) – each trying to touch "Sam". Being the size I am, I hadn't a chance. Simon was different. He just barged through and grabbed "Sam" with both hands. The Kerry captain had to wrestle it back from him.

Then I noticed Mum, whispering to Mr O'Sullivan. A bad feeling came over me. I noticed the camera in her hands. The feeling grew worse. The crowd was getting out of control. Mr Long appealed for order, but he was wasting his time. Mr O'Sullivan decided the visit of "Sam" was over. He guided his Kerry friend to the school gate – but not before he had grabbed hold of ME and dragged me through the gate with him. The gates were slammed shut. Mum appeared from nowhere with her camera.

Suddenly Mr O'Sullivan scooped me up in his huge hands and plopped me into the Sam Maguire Cup! Then he and the captain raised the Cup over their heads with a frightened me sitting in it, arms and legs hanging over the edge! Okay, I had grown a bit since the LAST time I was in the Cup (eight years ago) but I still fitted snugly into it!

And I was still scared, wobbling and waving when – FLASH! – Mum appeared with her camera.

"Beck-y! Beck-y!" the crowd chanted behind the gate.

FLASH! Mum took another photo to make sure . . . I was SO embarrassed! My face was more pink than Mr O'Sullivan's shirt. At last I managed to scramble out of the Cup – just in time to see Mum give Mr O'Sullivan a big kiss on the cheek . . . I felt I was going to collapse and die of shame there and then.

I came home from school in a real sulk. Mum was, of course, in one of her jolliest moods, singing along with a CD of Robbie Williams' greatest hits.

"How could you do that, Mum?"

"Do what, dear?"

"You know well. Embarrass me in front of the whole school – putting me in the Cup."

"Nonsense. They were all jealous of you. And

proud. Didn't you hear them chant 'Beck-y! Beck-y!'"

"But I didn't want to be in the Cup."

"Honestly, Becky – is that all the thanks I get? I had to persuade Mr O'Sullivan for ages – telling him how you had been in the Cup before – as a baby. I bet you are the only child in Ireland who has been in the Sam Maguire Cup TWICE! Honestly!"

"But it was in front of the whole school –"

"Well, I'm sorry that I couldn't arrange for the photograph to be taken in a quiet studio in town, but Sam Maguire had a train to catch. Honestly, Becky!"

"And you kissed Mr O'Sullivan – in front of the whole school!"

"Yes – because he was very helpful and understanding."

She plonked my dinner down in front of me – my favourite spaghetti bolognese.

"He's quite a hunk, isn't he?" she purred.

"MUM! That is gross!"

I don't think I will EVER eat spaghetti bolognese again.

23

A Disappointment and a Surprise

Mum produced the photograph the next day – just me in the Cup. I was actually waving to the crowd and not looking so frightened at all. I don't remember waving. Actually, to tell the truth, I thought I looked rather cute.

"I suppose it's not too bad," I admitted.

"Not too bad? It's brilliant," Mum squealed. "It's so brilliant I am going to have it enlarged and framed."

I knew from the look in her eye that there was no point in my protesting.

"And here's the other photo I took." This one had Mr O'Sullivan and the Kerry captain holding me aloft in the Cup.

"Equally brilliant! You are to bring that in to Mr

Hunky O'Sullivan with my . . . with my . . . with my thanks and best wishes."

"His name isn't Hunky, Mum. It's Murty."

"Murty? Aw, isn't that cute? Murty!"

She waltzed out of the room in a kind of dream. I wondered if I should talk to Dad about this . . .

Later that evening when I was struggling with my homework *("Ten little sums – should only take you fifteen minutes," Miss Lane had said. It's been nearly AN HOUR and I'm stuck at number eight . . .)* Mum came by again.

"Simple. Just multiply by five and then divide by two."

"Thanks, Mum!"

"Brains and beauty. It's just unfair I was given so much of both . . ." She suddenly changed her tone. "Actually Becky – there's another reason I took that photograph. It was for Grandad."

"How do you mean?"

"He's not coming over for Christmas."

I had this really empty feeling inside me, but I couldn't speak.

"He still misses Granny a lot and he thinks it might be better for him to stay in London. He has lots of good friends and neighbours there."

"But we could cheer him up here –"

"He has made his mind up, love. Maybe we'll get him over in the summer. That's why I thought we could make him a very special Christmas card with your photo in it. Isn't that a good idea?"

"Suppose so . . ."

"Good girl. Now, can you manage number nine?"

* * *

I felt really down for the next few days. I had been looking forward to Grandad's visit, to playing and talking football and learning more little tricks. I did talk to him on the phone – and told him how Seán Boylan remembered 'Jimmy the Shimmy' – but it just wasn't the same as having him here.

Christmas was going to be very ordinary. Dad would probably get more golfing gear for the golf he never plays. Mum would probably get (another) Robbie Williams DVD – "*Live at Central Park*". Shona would probably get more "genuine original wooden worry beads from Thailand" from Guess Who? (who bought them in the market for one euro). ET would hopefully get a single ticket to the Planet Zarga . . . only joking. And I suppose Becky would get a surprise. A football annual? The new Tottenham jersey? Ho-hum . . .

A Disappointment and a Surprise

But then, something unusual happened. It began with an ambulance arriving next door. Mrs Pratt became ill and was rushed to hospital. A few days before Christmas – the very day we got our Christmas holidays from school – Mr Pratt telephoned Mum to ask if he could see me for a little while. Mum was puzzled, but said yes, of course.

If Mum was puzzled I was even more troubled. Why would he want to see ME? Was I in BIG TROUBLE? Maybe he would accuse me of causing so much worry to his wife that I had made her ill . . .

It was a very nervous Becky that knocked on the Pratts' door that afternoon.

"Come in, Rebecca. Do come in. You're welcome!"

Mr Pratt guided me into the sitting room. I had never been in the Pratts' house before. The room was dark – and brown. Everything seemed to be brown – heavy brown curtains, brown patterned wallpaper, dark brown armchairs. The gloom was lightened by the dancing flames of a gas fire. Scotty lay curled up on a rug in front of the fire and totally ignored me.

"Take a seat, Rebecca. I won't keep you long. Your mother tells me you got your holidays today, so I expect you will want to be out enjoying your freedom."

I nodded nervously, not really knowing what to say.

"Now about the shed and the shelter, which you know about –"

"I'm s-sorry."

"It's all right, Rebecca. I know you didn't mean any harm and were just being curious. A little too curious maybe, but –"

I wished the big brown armchair would swallow me up.

"I just wanted to explain about Elsie – that's Mrs Pratt. You see, when she was a little girl – about your age – she lived in London. There was a great war on then, and very often there were air raids – bombs were dropped on London from German planes. Most people built an air raid shelter in their garden. Elsie was always pleading with her dad to build one but he never did. He used to joke that the Germans would never bomb his house because he had lots of German friends. But one night they did bomb it and Elsie lost her whole family – her mum, dad, two sisters, baby brother and her gran. All killed. Elsie was buried under rubble for two days before she was pulled out, barely alive. Ever since she has been terrified of explosions and nervous about war. Even though it was over sixty years ago and thankfully we are far away from war, she never got over that awful day and she still lives in fear of what might happen. That's why she insisted on building a bunker under the shed – and being ready for war, if it ever came . . . It gave her peace of mind. She has been nervous all her life, but she is a good person – and she has been very good to me . . ." He paused and gave a big sigh. "We were never blessed with children so I suppose she finds it hard to understand them sometimes. Scotty here – and her hydrangeas – they are her babies."

My mouth felt dry. I wanted to speak but the words wouldn't come.

"I really – am – sorry –" was all I could squeak out.

"Anyway I thought I should explain all this to you, before . . . before . . . You're a bright girl, Rebecca. I know you will understand."

"Yes. Yes – I do. Please tell Mrs Pratt how sorry I am."

"Of course I will. And now I have – we have – a little surprise for you! Something for Christmas!"

He moved to the darkest corner of the room and returned with a strangely-shaped package – quite a big package.

"This is from us – just to make up for being nuisances sometimes!"

Again I was speechless. I couldn't even think what was in the package.

"Come on," Mr Pratt urged. "Let's open it up and see if you like it!"

We both tore at the wrapping until the surprise was revealed. It was a mini-goal – tubular bars that locked together – complete with net.

"Oh, Mr Pratt. This is great – but it's too much. I couldn't –" I knew I COULD accept it but I felt I had to say the opposite.

"Nonsense. I know you and your little American friend love football. And if you use this goal there won't be so many balls ending up in our garden! Here, let me help you carry it and we'll assemble it in your garden."

He picked up the bars while I got the net.

"Please thank Mrs Pratt for me. Will she be home for Christmas?"

Mr Pratt paused in the middle of gathering the wrapping paper.

"No. No, Elsie won't be coming home . . . any more. That's what the doctors say." His voice was trembling. "So, you see – it doesn't matter about the bunker any more, does it?"

I followed him out the door to my own house.

24

The End

You are probably wondering why this chapter of my story is called "The End" even though it's not the last chapter. Don't worry – it will all become clear very, very soon (and no peeking at the end of the chapter to find out!).

Christmas came and went. It wasn't the same without Grandad. Everyone was amazed at the Pratts' surprise present. My family could not understand why the people I had tormented with lost footballs would give me such a wonderful present. And they would never understand because I would never tell Mrs Pratt's secret. Nor would Josh, who was equally amazed. "Awesome!" was all he would say.

I hate January. It is cold and miserable. The days are very short – little time for football in the evening!

And of course we are back at school writing about "Christmas Day in Our House" for Miss Lane. *" . . . and then we all pulled Christmas crackers. I won a key ring, a paper hat and a joke that said: Q. When is a door not a door? A. When it's ajar!"* BORING.

Eventually February came round and the football season re-opened. Mr O'Sullivan had us training hard twice a week. The under-twelves had been knocked out of their competition, so we were his only chance of glory. We played a practice match against the under-twelves. I thought this was a bit unfair as they were much bigger than us (and especially me). Luckily, Josh was marking me and, since we knew each other so well, everything was all right. Not for Mr O'Sullivan, though.

"Come on, Becky! This is not a tea-party! I didn't invite yourself and Josh out for a stroll and a chat!"

He then switched Josh with Colm, which was bad news for me. Colm is big and strong and doesn't talk when he is playing football. He just plays football. I don't think I touched the ball once while Colm was marking me. It was just unfair.

We were beaten heavily by the under-twelves but that wasn't the worst part. Near the end of the match Simon fell awkwardly and hurt his ankle. He hobbled off in great pain. That ruled him out of the semifinal against Saint Mark's. We were in trouble because Simon was easily the biggest and strongest player on our team. It was not a good sign.

* * *

March 13th eventually came around. The day of the semifinal. The 13th. Would it be unlucky for us? Not a good sign . . . As I made my way to school that morning, it began to rain. And rain and rain and rain. Cats and dogs, kittens and puppies. I hate the stuff, especially when we are playing football. It's because of my glasses. I keep having to wipe them so that I can see properly.

The morning dragged on. Miss Lane was droning on about fractions – something about quarters and eighths – while I was gazing out at the rain, wishing it would go away. When she asked a question I hadn't a clue about the answer.

"Oh Rebecca! Dreamland again! If we could only have ONE-EIGHTH of your attention, you could still have SEVEN-EIGHTHS to dream about football. That's not too much to ask, is it?"

"No, Miss."

We crawled on to lunchtime. The team had a half-day off to play Saint Mark's. We piled into four cars – driven by two teachers and two parents – and set off to the cheers of the rest of the school. The rain had eased off but there was still a fine drizzle coming down by the time we reached The Park. It was a day for gloves (fortunately I had brought mine) and not for glasses (unfortunately I needed mine).

Mr O'Sullivan gathered us into a huddle.

"Now, lads –" *(Hello? Ciara and Becky!)* – "this is the BIG ONE. We're one step away from Croke Park but it's a big step. At your best you'll beat these fellows – but that means *all* of you at your best. Just do the simple things well. It's not a day for fancy football. What are we, lads?"

"We're the Best."

"Didn't hear you!"

"WE'RE THE BEST!"

"Let's hear it, Goodwill!"

Goodwill, wearing a bright orange hat, launched into his song:

Ballybawn! Ballybawn!
We're the best you ever saw
With a Knick-Knack,Paddywhack
Give a dog a bone
Ballybawn!
We're out on our own!

"Okay, lads! Give it your best!" Mr O'Sullivan thundered. "Go, Ballybawn, go!"

The End

We gave each other "high fives" and raced to take up our positions. Saint Mark's had brought a busload of supporters with them. Already they had begun a noisy chant – "Mark's! Mark's! Mark's! Mark's!" We had two teachers and two parents. There was a twenty-four-hour sale in 'Dazzling Interiors', so Mum had to work.

One step away . . .

Here we go.

We got off to the worst possible start. Saint Mark's sent a high lobbing ball into our goalmouth. Rory couldn't hold it and it was scrambled over the line. Two minutes gone and we are a goal down. The "Mark's!" chant grew louder. The ball was like a bar of soap but we did not panic. The first time I got the ball I tried a solo run but the ball screwed off my boot and a Mark's defender won it back. I could hear Mr O'Sullivan screaming.

"Simple, Becky! Keep it simple!"

He was right. It wasn't a day for solo runs. It was ages before the ball came my way again. This time I hacked it ahead of me and raced after it. As I picked it up I noticed the orange hat moving towards goal. I drove the ball as hard as I could ahead of Goodwill. He raced on to it at speed and crashed home a great goal. This time the chanters were silent but Mr O'Sullivan was doing a war-dance on the sideline. I was proud of my pass – or my "assist" as Josh would call it. "Awesome!" he would say.

As the game went on, the conditions grew worse. A lot of slipping and sliding and plenty of mistakes. Scores were hard to get. I had a chance of a point but the ball was becoming heavier and my effort dropped into the goalkeeper's arms. Saint Mark's edged into a lead. We missed Big Simon at centre-field. Half-time: Saint Mark's 1–3, Ballybawn 1–1.

"Keep the heads!" Mr O'Sullivan repeated as he handed out orange segments. "Keep the heads, and keep it simple. It will be a low-scoring game so we must take our chances. What must we do?"

"Take our chances," we muttered as the drizzle gave way to rain again. Heavy rain.

"Didn't hear you!"

"TAKE OUR CHANCES!"

The second half was a nightmare – for both teams. The rain poured down. I was hoping the referee might abandon the match, because the longer it went on the less I could see. Figures became a blur and as jerseys grew more and more muddy, it was hard for me to tell friend from foe. Puddles began to appear on the pitch. Mr O'Sullivan was right about the low scoring. Each side only scored a point in the second half. Saint Mark's 1–4, Ballybawn 1–2.

The End

Then, with only minutes to go, the golden chance came.

I tried a ground shot but the goalkeeper collected it and cheekily danced past me on a solo run. When he attempted to pass the ball, Goodwill nipped in and dispossessed him. I was still standing in front of goal only ten metres out. Goodwill saw this and chipped a perfect pass to me. The goalkeeper was stranded . . . TAKE OUR CHANCES . . . I had the ball in front of an open goal. TAKE OUR CHANCES . . . a goal would win the match for us. It was too easy. As I steadied myself, a figure appeared from my right, out of the gloom. A defender, desperately trying to prevent a certain goal. He slid across in front of me, sending a spray of mud in my direction. SPLAT! A huge black blob came right at me and landed on my glasses. Everything was no longer a blur. It was totally black. I was blind. I panicked and kicked wildly at the ball.

Before I could scrape the mud off my glasses, the chanting of Saint Mark's supporters told me the worst. The ball had rolled harmlessly wide. I had missed a certain goal. I slumped into the muck. In the distance I heard a very rude word coming from Mr O'Sullivan. I could not blame him. I had let him and Ballybawn down. When the final whistle went a couple of minutes later I felt so cold and wet and miserable.

133

Super Becky had become Useless Specky Becky. For all my shimmies and solo runs I could not kick the ball into an empty net from ten metres. Useless. Useless. Useless. I didn't want to face my team mates and most especially Mr O'Sullivan. Tears were now washing the mud from my face.

One step away from Croke Park . . .

Now we were a million, million steps away.

It was truly The End.

25

Maybe Not The End, Actually

"Attention please! Attention please! Sorry for the interruption, teachers."

Miss Lane rolled her eyes upwards as Mr Long's voice crackled over the school radio.

"Just want to say congratulations to our under-ten footballers who gave a great display yesterday in awful conditions and were narrowly beaten by Saint Mark's. Mr O'Sullivan says they were all heroes and on a better day they would have won. So well done to all and here's to next year. Thank you."

Tracy was in like a shot with a plea to Miss Lane.

"Can we have homework off, Miss?"

"Why, Tracy?"

"For the – great display – by the under-tens."

"Not a chance. I'll be looking for a great display of homework on fractions instead."

The pain of losing wouldn't go away. I could still see the empty goal – and then the big blob of muck coming at me . . . Even though Mr O'Sullivan said nice things after the match I was hurting all the way home . . .

"Hard luck, lads. Ye tried your best. Can't do more than that. Awful conditions. Match shouldn't have been played but Saint Mark's wouldn't agree. And no blame to anyone for losing. We win as a team. We lose as a team. Rory might have dropped a ball but how many saves has he made over the season? Becky might have missed a goal but how many scores did she make over the season? And what about her pass to Goodwill for our goal? No blame. We win as a team. We lose as a team . . ."

It was nice of him to say it but how many believed it? I imagined I could hear the whispers behind my back . . .

"How did she miss? An open goal . . ."

"I could have scored with my eyes shut –"

"Well, Specky Becky couldn't!"

Giggles. Open laughter.

Maybe Not The End, Actually

They were right. How DID I miss? I panicked.

* * *

That miss haunted me for weeks. Again and again I
stood ten metres out from my mini-goal in our garden,
closed my eyes and kicked. And every time, EVERY
TIME, I scored. But I couldn't do it when I needed
to do it, when we were one step away from Croke
Park . . .

Specky Becky let everyone down.

The weeks slid by. Mr O'Sullivan brought the
news that Saint Mark's won the Primary Schools Cup
Final – in Croke Park. Just think – that could have
been US if only – if only Specky Becky had not
panicked . . .

"Attention please!"

The sudden crackle of the school radio always startled
us.

*"Just a couple of notices. Number one – School will
close at twelve thirty next Tuesday. Teachers' meeting.
Please tell your parents!"*

We gave a big cheer.

"Number two. Somebody left a tap running in Room 5 during lunchtime and caused a mess. Please be more careful, children."

We didn't dare look at Simon.

"And finally, would Goodwill, Rory and Rebecca from Miss Lane's class report to the office NOW. Thank you!"

My heart was racing as the three of us made for the principal's office. What trouble were we in now?

"No trouble," Goodwill said. "It's probably the Manchester United scout – he wants to sign us up!"

"He's hardly going to sign *me* up!" I muttered.

"Come in! Come in!" Mr Long barked. "Oh, it's the three All-Stars!"

All-Stars? What did he mean? Mr O'Sullivan stood by the window. Mr Long held a letter in his hand.

"Don't look so worried, Rebecca! Here, I'll let Mr O'Sullivan explain."

He handed the letter to Mr O'Sullivan.

"Very simple, lads." *(Thank you, Mr O'Sullivan. I'm over here.)* "Every year the people who run the Primary Schools League choose a team from Dublin Schools to play in an exhibition match at half-time

138

during a big match in Croke Park. An All-Stars team – to show how good you are! This year it's the turn of the under-tens and you three lads *(Grrr!)* have been chosen from this school. Congratulations!"

It took a while to realise what he had just said.

"You mean," I stammered, "*we* are going – to play – in – Croke Park?"

"Yes, Becky. At half-time during the Dublin-Meath match in June. Your dream has come true, Becky!"

We whooped our way back down the corridor until heads appeared in doorways and told us to shush. When we told Miss Lane, Tracy wasted no time.

"Can we have homework off, Miss?"

"Why, Tracy?"

"To celebrate our three All-Stars."

"Oh all right. Just this once!"

Sometimes even Miss Lane can surprise us.

"Why, that's fantastic!" Mum cried on hearing the news. She really was excited. "Imagine! My little Becksy-Wecksy *(Grrr!)* playing in Croke Park. I can't wait to tell Grandad. I told you it was in the blood."

Even Dad was excited and promised he would go to cheer me on. Shona couldn't understand why Josh wasn't picked *(He's OVER ten, dumbbell)* so that Josh and Becks, the deadly duo, could star in Croke

Park. As for ET, he thinks he has discovered a lost planet . . .

* * *

I thought June 6th would never come. A week beforehand, I got a card from Grandad wishing me good luck and "make sure you show off your shimmy!" If only he could be there to see me.

At last the Great Day arrived. A beautiful warm sunny day – no wet blurry glasses! Mr O'Sullivan collected the three All-Stars and brought us to Croke Park. Mum told me to be sure and wave to her in the Hogan Stand. (*Sure, Mum. No problem. You'll only be one of THOUSANDS there.*)

Thousands! I couldn't believe my eyes. Mr O'Sullivan said there were *sixty thousand* people there. Sixty thousand people would be watching US! ME! We watched the opening minutes of the Dublin-Meath match before we had to go downstairs to change. The noise was unbelievable. I began to feel nervous. Playing in front of six or (at best) sixteen people was one thing but sixty thousand . . . We were given a Dublin strip to wear – blue jersey, navy togs, blue socks. I got the number twelve jersey. Mr O'Sullivan was co-manager of the Dublin team. He gave me a big wink.

"Show them your stuff, Becky!"

As we lined up alongside the Meath All-Stars I noticed there were two girls on the Meath team. I was the only girl on our side. I felt proud. A great burst of applause from overhead signalled that it was half-time.

"Right lads – and lassies!" *(At last! Thank you, Mr O'Sullivan!)* "You're on!"

We marched out proudly as the announcer explained to the crowd who we were – "The cream of under-tens from Dublin and Meath schools". We got a huge cheer. This was unbelievable. I was marching out to play in Croke Park before sixty thousand people (well, all right – fifty thousand – Mr O'Sullivan said ten thousand would be gone to the shops or the toilets).

As we marched along the sideline I heard one man shout –

"Look! Look at the wee one with the glasses. Number Twelve. That's what our fellows need – glasses. Kicked twelve wides in the first half. My granny could do better!"

I looked into the Hogan Stand but it was a sea of faces. Then, above all the din, I heard a familiar voice screaming.

"Becky! Becky! Over here!"

It was Mum, frantically waving. She was only

about ten rows back. And there was Dad beside her, giving me a "thumbs-up" sign. And beside him was – no, it couldn't be true! Beside him was GRANDAD! They never told me! Grandad stood up and did a little shimmy. I waved excitedly at the three of them. I would HAVE to play the game of my life for them – and for Mr O'Sullivan.

I *know* it was only a ten-minute game and I *know* it was played across the field into special goals, but to me it didn't matter. This was Croke Park, where great matches were played, where great players had played, where my grandad had played. This was not dreamtime. This was the real thing. Croke Park. Sixty thousand people watching, or maybe fifty thousand. I bent down to touch the grass I had imagined skipping along for so long. Here we go.

Ten minutes is a very short time and it goes very fast in a game of football in Croke Park, but I enjoyed every one of those minutes. The ball came my way. A little solo run. A defender in my way. A shimmy and I was past him. A shot. A point. I had scored a point in Croke Park! There was a great cheer for the "wee one with the glasses". I saluted towards the Hogan Stand. Grandad would have enjoyed *that*! I was loving every second of this. Meath scored a goal at the other end – big Meath cheer! – but straight away the ball came up to Goodwill who lashed it into the net. Even bigger Dublin cheer! The crowd were loving this, cheering every slick move, every good catch. Time was running out. Goodwill caught a ball out on the wing. Two, three defenders closed in on him. Bad mistake, lads! Goodwill slid a perfect pass along the ground to the "wee one with the glasses". The deadly Ballybawn duo! This time there would be no mistake. No mud in your eye. Croke Park. Sunshine. Sixty thousand. Grandad. *Go, Becky, go!*

It was perfectly placed. Along the ground. Into the corner. Goalkeeper never had a chance. A huge roar from the crowd. Another salute to the Hogan Stand. I was walking on air. Even tried a Robbie Keane cartwheel. Goodwill raced up and gave me a big hug. Final whistle. Cheers. Applause. A big pair of hands grabs me and raises me aloft. It's Mr O'Sullivan.

"Proud of you, Becky! Proud of you!"

This is all so unreal. Will I wake up and discover it was a dream? No. This really happened. I played in Croke Park. Before sixty thousand people. And I scored a goal and a point. And Grandad – 'Jimmy the Shimmy' – was there to see it.

Dreams do come true, after all.

THE END

By the author of *The Summer of Lily & Esme,*
winner of The Bisto Book of the Year Award.

DUCK & SWAN

John Quinn

When Martin 'Duck' Oduki, abandoned in Dublin by a
Nigerian father and Irish mother, runs away from St Mark's
Care Centre, Emer Healy discovers him hiding on a school
bus bound for Galway.

Watching her sick mother's struggle to regain her health,
Emer is also running from the pain and confusion she feels
inside. It isn't long before the two children discover they need
each other.

Duck finds other unusual allies in Granny Flynn, who knows
a thing or two about institutional life, and her husband, blind
Tom, who introduces Duck to the game of hurling.

Duck and Swan is a moving and often funny story of
friendship and acceptance set against a background of
intolerance and high adventure in a quiet part of County
Galway.

ISBN 978-1-85371-317-0

winner of The Bisto Book of the Year Award.

The Summer of
Lily
&
ESME

John Quinn

What a summer it is for Alan! He wasn't much looking forward to living in the country, not after spending all of his life in Dublin. And when he finds that his next-door neighbours are two very old ladies, he is not much happier.

Then he finds a mysterious locked room in his house and hears about the ghost of a boy called Albert who died tragically. When Lily and Esme, the two old ladies, start calling him Albert, he begins to get worried but is determined to solve the mystery.

With the help of his new friend, Lisa, and some friendly grown-ups, he unearths the story of another summer seventy years before and is at last able to give his new friends their dearest wish. *The Summer of Lily & Esme* is both moving and funny.

ISBN 978-1-85371-162-6